LYLA

THROUGH MY EYES: NATURAL DISASTER ZONES

Hotaka (Japan)

Shaozhen (China)

Lyla (New Zealand)

Angel (Philippines)

THROUGH MY EYES

Shahana (Kashmir)

Amina (Somalia)

Naveed (Afghanistan)

Emilio (Mexico)

Malini (Sri Lanka)

Zafir (Syria)

THROUGH MY EYES NATURAL DISASTER ZONES

series editor Lyn White

LYLA

FLEUR BEALE

First published by Allen & Unwin in 2018

Allen & Unwin
83 Alexander Street
Crows Nest NSW 2065
Australia
Phone: (61 2) 8425 0100
Email: info@allenandunwin.com
Web: www.allenandunwin.com

A Cataloguing-in-Publication entry is available from the
National Library of Australia
www.trove.nla.gov.au

ISBN 978 1 76011 378 0

For teaching resources, explore www.allenandunwin.com/resources/for-teachers

Cover and text design by Sandra Nobes
Cover photos: portrait of girl by PhotoAlto/Alamy Stock Photo; cathedral by New Zealand Defence Force/Wikimedia Commons; crack in bridge by NigelSpiers/Shutterstock.com; damage on bridge by Robin Bush/Getty.
Set in 11/15 pt Plantin by Midland Typesetters, Australia
This book was printed in June 2022 by SOS Print + Media

10 9 8 7 6

The paper in this book is FSC® certified. FSC® promotes environmentally responsible, socially beneficial and economically viable management of the world's forests.

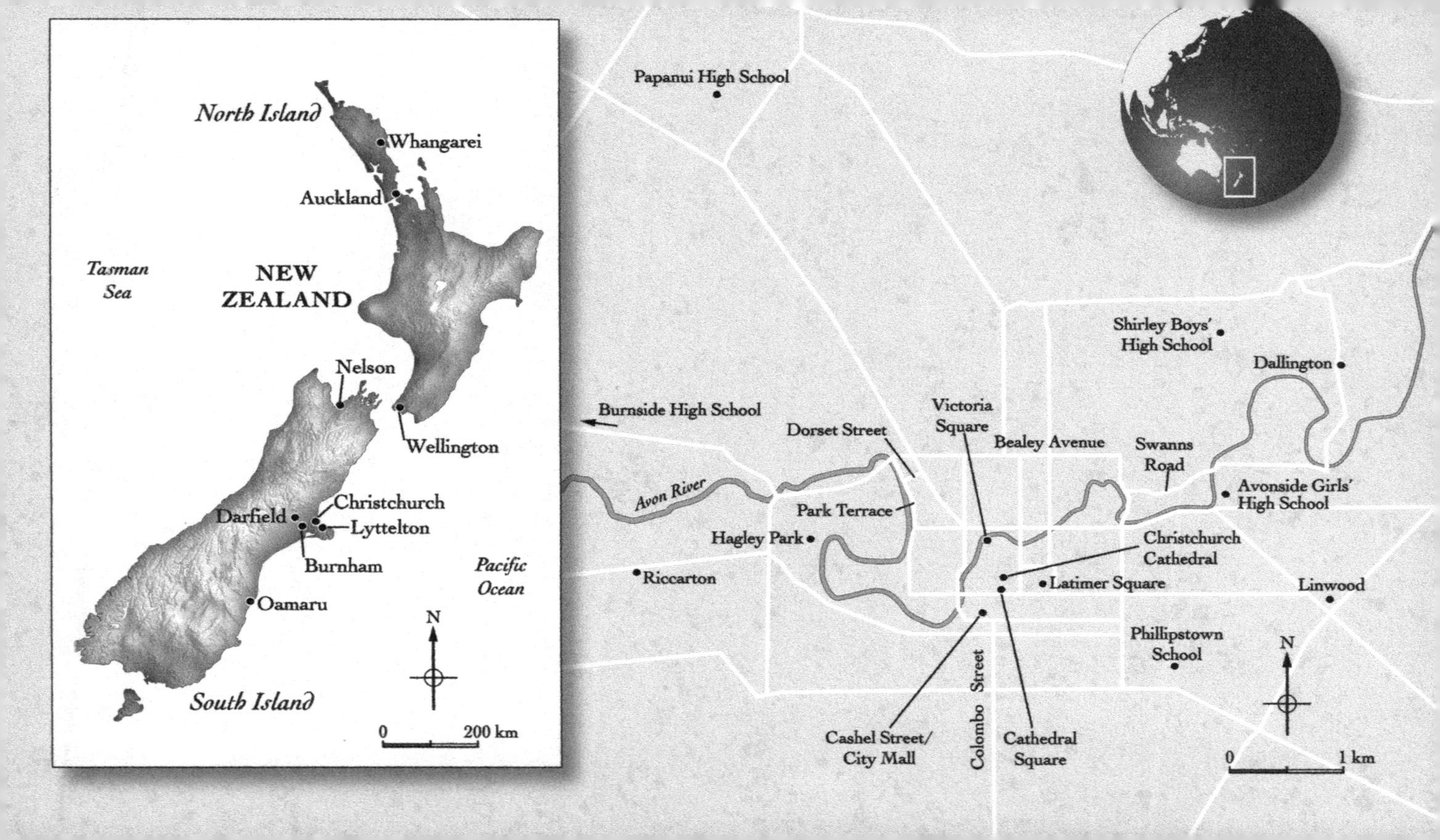
North Island
Whangarei
Auckland
Tasman Sea
NEW ZEALAND
Nelson
Wellington
Christchurch
Darfield
Lyttelton
Burnham
Pacific Ocean
Oamaru
South Island
N
0
200 km
Papanui High School
Burnside High School
Shirley Boys' High School
Dallington
Victoria Square
Dorset Street
Bealey Avenue
Swanns Road
Avonside Girls' High School
Avon River
Park Terrace
Hagley Park
Christchurch Cathedral
Riccarton
Latimer Square
Linwood
Phillipstown School
Colombo Street
Cashel Street/ City Mall
Cathedral Square
N
0
1 km

One

School was out, the sun was shining and I didn't have babysitting duty until six o'clock. Hmm, I'd better remind Shona and Katie not to go home without me. I grabbed my phone.

Meet you outside GG Block.

Other people called it Main Block but we called it GG Block in honour of my great-grandmother because she'd been head girl at Avonside Girls' a million years ago. The building was like a symbol of endurance for me because the big September earthquake hadn't killed it thanks to the strengthening done at the end of last century. True, the whole place was a bit broken and we weren't allowed inside until more work was done, but it for sure wasn't busted. She was a red-brick, two-storeyed grand old lady, gracious and tough.

It had survived the zillions of aftershocks since September, too. Can you call buildings resilient? Yeah, why not? The whole country kept saying, *OMG those Christchurch people, their city is munted but look at them – they're so resilient.* GG Block wasn't munted; therefore it must be resilient. Good logic there, Lyla!

But I was sick of being resilient. In my opinion, the resilient-sayers should try living here in Christchurch, City of Shaky Ground. My message to the God of Earthquakes was: *Hey, Rūaumoko! It's February now and you've been shaking us for five months. Enough already! Go back to sleep. Please.*

Ugh! Quake memories. Quick! Think of something else. Yes! Saved by an incoming text from Katie.

C U in 5.

I wandered through the crowd of girls milling around on the big lawn at the front of the school where we always met up, trying to decide where to park myself. Nobody seemed to be in a hurry to get home. A group sprawled under one of the trees, others gossiped at picnic tables. Joanne from my class waved me over. 'Lyla, Mum can pick us up from Swanns Road bridge tomorrow if you like.'

'Tell her she's a star! You sure you don't want to come into town with us?'

She shook her head. 'Love to, but Mum's dragging me to the eye-man. I won't be out of there until about one-thirty.'

'Want some help choosing new frames? Just in case your mum thinks granny glasses are the way to go.' Joanne's mum wouldn't, though. I'd known her forever because they lived in Linwood not far from us, and she was one styly woman.

Joanne suddenly looked a lot more cheerful. 'That'd

be awesome! Then I can escape and hit town with you guys.'

I put the appointment details in my phone.

Katie and Shona appeared only two minutes after they said they would – a record. Shona was stomping her way across the grass and venting about something, judging by the way she was tugging at her frizzy hair – trying to untangle the hair band from her ponytail would be my guess. Katie, as always, looked put-together and unruffled. It could have had something to do with being constructed along model lines, plus the fact that she liked her hair to know its place, which was pretty much always in two long plaits.

'Why aren't you at kapa haka practice?' Katie dumped her bag on the grass and slid in beside me.

Shona snapped, 'Cancelled till next week. She told us that already, just like she told us about no sprog-sitting.'

I grinned at her. 'What's got your knickers in a knot? Don't tell me drama sucks!'

She shook her head. 'No, drama's great. It's Greer. I just wish she'd finish her wretched thesis and go flatting. My sister the stress queen. Take a look at this!' She held out her phone.

Katie and I bent over it, shading the screen to read the text that had thrown Shona into grump-land. *Get me another USB. Urgent!! I'm depending on you. Don't let me down.*

'Oops!' I said. 'That's Blake's fault. He told her having only two back-ups for something as important as her PhD thesis was just asking for trouble.' He was totally OTT about it even though she had everything backed up on a separate hard drive and another back-up on a USB she wore round her neck including when she went to bed. My bro was in his second year at uni studying computing, so figured he was an expert.

Shona heaved a sigh. 'He's right, I guess, and I wouldn't mind, but that text is so rude. *And* she threw a *fit* at me this morning.'

Katie stood up. 'We'll be grateful to her when she invents some amazing sustainable house and saves the planet. But for now, anyone fancy a snack at mine?'

That would be yes. Katie lived just across the Avon River, and Shona and I always left our bikes at Katie's house so we could all walk to school together. We took our time; it was pretty by the river. But when we had to cross the bridge we didn't linger – it was closed to traffic since it got damaged in September but was safe enough for pedestrians, so they told us.

'Is Greer worried she's going to fail?' I asked once we were back on steady-ish ground.

Shona shrugged. 'Yeah. She won't, though. She's been getting really positive feedback from her supervisor. An eco house-building firm read an article she wrote and wants to interview her, too. But her thesis is due in really soon and she's driving Mum and me crazy.'

'She'll calm down once she's handed it in,' I said. Greer was cool. She'd often hung out with the three of us, ever since we were about eleven and didn't need a babysitter but our picky parents wouldn't let us be on our own. 'But speaking of annoying things, I've got to move into Blake's room for an entire week.'

Katie tipped her head to one side in her Query Pose. 'Wellington grands, or Queensland?'

'Wellington. It's Mum's fortieth tomorrow.' I was actually looking forward to spending the week with my grandparents – it would be perfect if I didn't have to share room space with Blake.

Shona, still snippy, said, 'Betcha Blake won't be doing any of the adrenalin stuff you've got planned.'

'Not my bro,' I said. 'He says he's going to take snaps of the grands' faces when Mum's teetering up on the high ropes.'

Blake wasn't into adventure, but nothing much bothered him either. He was very Zen about the earthquakes, too, even though the big September one had thrown him out of bed. He just said that's what can happen when you live in a city built above a fault line and it decides to do a bit of stretching and bending.

Myself, I blamed Twitchy-Earth God Rūaumoko for all the damage to my city. You can talk to a god, but a fault line – not so much.

Katie unlocked her front door. There was a note on the floor. *Katie, be an angel and collect the kids from school. And if you can find my phone I'll love you forever.*

Neither of those requests was unusual. Katie backed out the door saying, 'Make the toast. Unless you'd rather have yesterday's bread.'

Her half-brother and sister were five and almost seven, quite cute and quite loud. There would be the usual mayhem when they arrived home in a race with Katie, which she sometimes made them lose – to show them life was a struggle.

She let them win today. We put toast in front of them so it was almost quiet when we heard the dull roar of an earthquake. If we'd been by ourselves we'd have waited to see if evasive action was needed, but we weren't by ourselves so we slid under the table with the kids. The house shook. The five-year-old yelled, 'Do the turtle! Keep safe!' Both of them curled up on their knees, one hand protecting their heads and the other clutching a table leg, foreheads resting on the floor.

'It's stopped now,' Shona said. 'I'm guessing a three point eight.'

The Christchurch guessing game: *what's the strength of the aftershock?*

The kids guessed five point one, and four point five.

Katie ruffled their hair. 'Let's see what the computer says.' She checked the geonet site. 'Shona, you're spot on.'

We were all fed up with playing Rūaumoko's guessing game. How many more times was the earth going to shake?

Two

When I got home Mum greeted me with a hug – and a not so subtle reminder that I'd be sharing with Blake. 'I've made up all the beds for tomorrow, Lyla.'

'So kind! But I'm not sleeping in Blake's room tonight. Nana Kiri won't mind.' My grandmother always slept in my bed and she wouldn't mind day-old sheets. She was very Zen about things, just like Blake.

Mum waved a hand. 'Fine by me.'

I took myself off next door to my babysitting job. Henry, aged six, and Leo, eight, weren't bad kids, but they were pretty spooked these days by the shaky earth. Their mum, Natalie, tilted her head towards the boys. Uh oh, the spooked-kids tilt.

I gave her my competent child-carer nod and she left after a kiss for each of the boys. She was a receptionist at a medical centre, and evening shifts were only a problem when her hubby Don was travelling like he was right now, doing agricultural advising.

'Show me where Dad is today,' I said to the kids.

They raced to the map on the wall. Henry plonked a finger in the middle of South America. 'Here.'

Leo landed on Buenos Aires. 'Mum says we can get out of school and go to the airport to meet him.'

'Yeah,' Henry said. 'He'll be here in four more sleeps.'

'How about we make him welcome-home cards?'

It was a good idea – they hardly noticed a minor shake happening among the glue, glitter and spelling glitches.

They were in bed all tucked up and asleep by nine o'clock – something of a record these days. Well done, Lyla! I was deep into my homework when a text arrived from Nana Kiri. ***Would Clemmie like a replacement china shepherdess for her birthday? I've seen the exact same one!!!***

Clemmie being my mum, who reckoned the only good thing to come out of the September quake was the shattering of that stupid statue. For a second, I thought about texting back *She'd be thrilled!!* But no, I couldn't be that mean – mainly because I'd have to live with Mum's reproachful sighs forever after.

Truthfully, not her thing. She needs trainers, size 39. Keeps borrowing mine.

I added a link to shoes I'd be happy to own if Mum didn't like them.

Thanks, Lyla. See you tomorrow. We get in at 2.30. Remind Clemmie!!! Xxxx

Nana Kiri always said that, ever since Mum didn't

pick them up on time years ago. I forget the reason, but it would have been a valid one – a gunman on the loose, or maybe a lost toddler. I could have gone to the airport with Mum to meet them, but I had other plans for the afternoon, thanks to school finishing at midday so that all secondary teachers could have a union meeting. Go, unions!

Pops and Nana Kiri didn't usually fly down from Wellington for Mum's birthday, but apparently turning forty is huge. So on Tuesday the twenty-second of February we'd booked a posh restaurant for a family dinner in town. The rest of the birthday celebrations had already been organised by super-planners Dad, Blake and me, even though my bro and the grands wouldn't be doing any of it. They preferred to keep their feet on the ground.

I often looked at my grandparents and couldn't figure out how two such gentle people could produce an adrenalin junkie like my mum. It was a mystery – and I knew they worried about her being a cop.

Dad was a trauma nurse in Christchurch Hospital's emergency department, so pretty much into the adrenalin too. And I got Blake's share of that gene as well as my own.

Breakfast Tuesday morning with both parents taking the day off was an Event. Dad made fritters from the frozen whitebait he'd secretly thawed overnight. I made pancakes. Blake got out of bed in time to join in the eating part, but I guess he'd have got up anyway because lectures had started for the year.

Mum opened her present from Dad, Blake and me – vouchers for a gliding trip and a high ropes course, although to be honest that was because I wanted to be up in the treetops on a skinny rope high above the ground. For a second she just stared as if she couldn't believe what she was seeing, then she leapt to her feet. 'I'm going gliding! I really am! Wow, you fantastic, wonderful people. It's the best present. I absolutely love it!'

Dad leant towards me and Blake to stage whisper, 'Do you think she likes it? Is she just pretending?'

Mum didn't even hear – I reckon her head was already somewhere up in the stratosphere.

Blake asked, 'So what are you guys going to do with your day off?'

Dad nodded towards Mum. 'Jean Batten there is meeting up with a couple of old school friends this morning. Some fancy café in town.'

I reached across the table to prod his chest. 'Which leaves you free to drool over fancy cars in Fazazz. Right?'

He grinned. 'I might take a bit of a look. Just for ten minutes.'

More like ten hours – Dad'd live at Fazazz if he could. Mum came back down from the stratosphere. 'What are you doing with your free afternoon, daughter mine?'

I gave a summary of my plans. 'Catching a ride into town. Hitting the mall. Hanging out.'

Mum fixed me with a glare. 'Who's driving you? What type of licence is she on?'

Oh, the joy of having a cop for a mother. 'Joanne's mum. Sorry, I should have asked her for a photo of her licence.'

She patted my head and grinned.

'But I won't be biking, so I could use a ride to school, Mummy dearest, Daddy darling.'

Blake made puking noises.

Dad regarded me across the table, his face wearing a suspiciously calculating look. I beat him to it. 'Okay! I'll do the dishes if you'll take me to school.'

He laughed. 'Deal. And it's cooler today. Dress appropriately.' Dad in Health Monitor mode.

Peace, harmony and happy birthday-ness. All we needed now to make it perfect was a whole day without earthquakes.

Three

We got to the designated pick-up point just as Joanne's mother pulled up. 'Colombo Street lights okay, you lot?'

'Sure. Great. Thanks.'

Joanne spent the trip swivelled around helping to plan what we'd do once she was free from the eye-man.

Her mother dropped the three of us off at the lights. I pointed ahead of us to Victoria Square. 'Look – they're putting the Chinese New Year lanterns in the trees.'

We watched for a minute or two before wandering on to the centre of town where Cathedral Square still had displays from the Festival of Flowers. A couple of tourists knelt behind an elephant made of wire and greenery, trying to get a picture of it with the cathedral in the background.

'Sweet,' Shona said.

'Lots of tourists around,' Katie said. We scuttled out of the way of a Japanese man with a thousand cameras round his neck lining up a shot of the cathedral. He looked to be having trouble getting the spire and the rose window in the same shot.

'I hope they fix it soon,' Shona said. 'It'll be good to be able to go inside again.'

I laughed at her. 'And you were such a regular churchgoer!'

She gave me a shove. 'You know what I mean. That cathedral – it's the heart of Christchurch.'

Katie started walking. 'Yeah. True. But I need food. Let's do it.'

She towed us down High Street until I hauled her to a stop. 'Not the food hall.' I waved my hand at the sky. 'The sun's out. It's a sit-outside day, not a food hall day.'

'There won't be any empty benches,' Shona said. 'Look around you, Lyla. The whole city's in town today.'

'Fine! You go to the food hall. Come and find me on my sunny bench.' We kept walking and arguing – food hall or sun. Sun or food hall.

But we didn't get to the food hall. We were still walking down the mall when the world around us shook itself to bits.

We were used to aftershocks. This time when the shaking started, for a nanosecond we thought it was just another one – nothing to worry about.

It wasn't just another one. The shaking knocked us off our feet before we had time to panic, yell or think about what we should do. We huddled together as much as we could with the ground going crazy beneath us.

I don't remember hearing screaming. I had no breath for screaming. I remember jagged thoughts – *it's never going to stop. We're going to die. Stop. Please. Just stop.*

But the ground didn't listen to prayers or pleas or screams. It just kept on bucking and buckling and heaving. So much noise. Earthquakes are loud. The earth shrieks as it tears itself apart. Buildings moan before they give up and crash to the ground.

This time the noise and shaking seemed to go on forever. Fifteen seconds felt like fifteen years. And when it did stop we were in an alien place full of chaos.

For seconds after the ground quieted we waited, not believing it was over, before we clambered to our feet. I didn't trust the ground. I expected it to go crazy all over again. We looked at each other and maybe my eyes were wide and shocked just like my friends' were. I wiped at blood on Katie's neck with my finger. 'You okay?'

She shook her head. 'Yes. No. I'm still alive. I think.'

'It's foggy,' Shona said. 'Why is it foggy?'

We couldn't see much through the swirling fog but we could hear buildings all around the mall collapsing and dying, their bones shattered. Car alarms and building alarms shrieked, all adding to the racket.

'The buildings. They're falling down.' Shona scrabbled for her phone. 'I've got to call Greer. Mum'll be okay, but...'

'There'll be aftershocks.' Katie grabbed our hands. 'Let's get out of here. Greer will be fine. It won't help if you get yourself killed.'

Mum? Dad? Blake? Was Joanne okay?

We stumbled along over the uneven road. There were sirens now. I tasted grit. The white stuff in the air wasn't fog, it was dust. I looked around. There were lots of people.

So much dust. It swirled and lifted in great clouds. Sheets of paper from shattered offices flew and fluttered. I couldn't see up or down the street, but the dust didn't hide the destruction on both sides of us.

Katie headed towards the square. 'Come on.'

It was what we'd been told, time and again: *head for open space away from buildings.*

Shona was crying. 'There must be people under the rubble.'

The Japanese man? The giggling couple behind the elephant? How many others? Were they hurt – or worse?

A woman holding a toddler's hand stumbled along through the rubble a few steps ahead of us. They were both crying. 'Why isn't she carrying him? She should be carrying him.'

Shona tried to hold me back. 'No, Lyla! We have to go home. Follow the quake plan.'

'I will. But I'll just…' I caught up with the woman and saw she was very pregnant.

I picked her kid up, tears, snot and all. She took hold of my arm too. 'Thank you. I can't…'

'It's okay,' I said. 'What's his name?'

'Eli.'

Eli put his arms around my neck and hung on. Great. Survive an earthquake and suffer death by toddler.

Up ahead, Katie stopped. Her voice floated back on the dust. 'The cathedral! The spire's gone.'

The air had cleared enough to give a view down the street to the square. She was right. The spire wasn't there. It lay on the ground, just a pile of rubble now.

I couldn't bear to look at it. There had to be people under those heavy stones.

I led the woman to a bench. She took Eli onto her lap. 'Thank you.'

'Will you be okay? D'you want...'

'We'll be all right now. My husband – we'd arranged to meet here at one o'clock.' She pulled out her phone. 'It's nearly that now.'

But it looked as though she was only just holding it together. Her face was pale and strained. It was the tear tracks through the dust on her cheeks that got to me. She shouldn't be by herself.

'I'll wait with you.' I took out my own phone.

'The network's jammed.'

'Like September.' I sent texts to both parents and Blake. *I'm ok. You?* It could be hours before they got them and hours before I got theirs. If... *don't go there.*

The square was a mass of people, ghostly shapes in the dust. I couldn't see Shona or Katie. A man stood near us, his hands over his face and blood pouring down his fingers. I jumped up and ran to him. 'Come over here. Sit down.'

He came with me, as if on automatic pilot. The woman patted the bench beside her. 'Sit with us.'

Weird. It seemed to help her, being able to do

something for somebody else. He peered at me through bloody fingers. 'Thank you, young lady.'

He wasn't doing a good job of stopping the bleeding. Even less when he dropped one hand to steady himself on the bench. The woman took it. She didn't seem to mind the blood and she didn't seem to understand he needed more help than just having his hand held. I'd have to do it.

Apply pressure to stop a wound bleeding. But if I put my hand over the cut, germs would get in. Both my hands felt gritty from the dust, and they sure hadn't been sterile before the earth moved. But he was going to bleed to death if somebody didn't do something. The woman – if she'd had a nappy bag for Eli once, she didn't have it now. There was nothing I could use for a dressing.

'Move your hand,' I told him. 'You need more pressure on that.' He dropped his hand and blood spurted. The cut was jagged and it looked deep. *Please, don't let him die.* I pressed my palm over the wound, then wriggled around to stand behind him. 'Lean back. It's okay. I've got you.'

At a rough guess he was in his seventies – about the same age as Grandy. How much blood had he already lost? I wanted Katie and Shona. We needed help, but nobody seemed to see us. I looked towards the police kiosk – it seemed undamaged and people were milling around it, but nobody even glanced at us.

Eli's mother was talking. 'It's all right,' she kept saying to the man. 'You're okay. You're going to be all right.'

Another wicked aftershock hit. First the roar, then the shaking. My hand flew off the man's head. I was on my knees, and I wanted to scream and scream and never stop screaming. Eli did scream. Blood cascaded from the man's head. More bricks and chunks of concrete peeled themselves from high on buildings.

The woman was shouting. 'It's all right, Eli. We're safe. Don't cry. It's okay. We're safe.'

We weren't safe and we never would be ever again.

The man moaned. I lurched to my feet. 'Lie down. You'll be safer lying down.' I almost tugged him off the bench, slapping a hand against his wound – so much blood. I tried to wriggle out of my cardigan to make him a pillow and discovered I was still wearing my backpack. The woman pulled herself together enough to help me take it off.

A man running past stopped. 'I'm a doctor. Let's have a look at you.' But there wasn't anything he could do that we weren't already doing. He didn't have any supplies either. 'Keep the pressure on that wound. Don't let him go to sleep. Somebody'll be along eventually to take him to hospital.'

How long would it take somebody to come? I didn't want to stay. I wanted to find Mum and Dad. Blake was at uni – I just had to hope he wasn't hurt, that the shaking wasn't so bad out at Ilam. Here it felt like we were on a trampoline that just kept bouncing.

Katie and Shona would be following their family quake plans by now. *Go home. Wait there. Stay safe.* I should go home too. That's what I was supposed to do. I didn't want to be here with a bleeding man and a woman who might give birth at any second. She shifted on the bench, wincing. 'Hey! The baby's not coming, is it?'

She gave a tiny laugh. 'No. I promise.'

Sirens. The throb of helicopters. Cracking followed by crashing as more masonry gave up and fell. Dust and grit and sheets of paper.

People walked by, faces blank with shock. A couple of boys in Boys' High uniforms ran towards each other, arms out to crush each other in a hug. Still nobody stopped with offers of help.

A policeman strode through the crowd shouting, 'Hagley Park. Go to Hagley Park. Keep going. Hagley Park.'

I ached to get up and join the tide of shocked, dusty people walking away from the desperate city. It was cold now. I wished the sun would come out again. I wished my cardigan wasn't under the man's head. His eyes were shut. The woman kept talking to him. She asked him his name.

'Ian.' Long pause. 'Ian MacKenzie.'

'Don't go to sleep, Ian MacKenzie. You're going to be okay, but you have to stay awake.'

He said something, or it could have been just a moan.

She took it for an answer. 'Good. You're doing well, Ian. My name's Selina. And this is…'

'Lyla.'

Her husband arrived. He put his arms around his family. Tears from both of them. He squatted down to check Ian. 'I'll get help. There's triage setting up in Latimer Square.' Eli wailed as his father ran away.

Cathedral Square emptied. Eli watched the helicopters. Selina talked to Ian, nagging until he made a noise in response. I couldn't think of anything to say to him. I was so cold. A woman hurried towards us, her arms full of a pile of white hotel bathrobes. She gave us one each. 'It's getting chilly now.' She was gone before we could thank her.

Blood gushed as soon as I took the pressure off the wound. I slapped my hands back in place. Selina wrapped the robe around my shoulders and wiped blood from Ian's face with it. It made a difference, being warm.

The ground kept shaking. Selina's husband came back with men carrying a door. They lifted Ian onto it and told me to walk beside him. 'Keep the pressure on as much as you can.'

I tried, but blood ran out from under my hand. My mind kept skipping ahead. Dad would be doing triage in Latimer Square. Mum would be helping people but I couldn't guess where she'd be.

It was only two blocks from Cathedral Square to Latimer Square – but it was two blocks over broken roads filled with rubble and shocked people. Aftershocks kept the ground unsteady. I could only hold one hand pressed to Ian's head. I hoped it would be enough.

We got there. The men lowered the door to the ground. One of them put an arm round my shoulders in a brief hug. 'Well done, but you go home now, eh.'

A woman bent over Ian. 'We'll take over now. Good work.' She had an Aussie accent.

'Will he be okay?' I could only whisper.

She didn't raise her eyes from Ian's bloody head. 'Hope so. Time will tell. At least he's got a chance, thanks to you.'

He had to be all right. He had to live. I stepped away to look around me. The square thronged with people: the injured, the helpers and those like me who were searching for family. The ground rolled. People screamed.

My parents weren't there.

Four

Where were Mum and Dad? Why hadn't they told me where they were going for lunch? I should have asked. I should have gone home with Shona and Katie. I felt utterly alone in this alien, ruined city.

Somebody, a policeman maybe, shouted to clear the square: the authorities were setting up an emergency response centre.

I started walking, one of a river of people leaving the city behind. Some of them limped, some bled from cuts. Bare-footed women carried their high-heeled shoes. Some of them ran – shoes in one hand, phones in the other.

I stopped, trying to remember what my parents had said about their plans this morning when the world was still safe.

A man put his hand on my arm. 'You okay there?'

I shook my head. 'My parents, my brother – I don't know where they are.' I couldn't say any more.

He winced. 'I know the feeling – but the best thing

you can do is go home. Keep yourself safe. They'll be expecting you to do that.'

'Yes. Thanks.'

'Want me to walk with you?'

His kindness helped steady me. 'I'm okay. Thanks though. I hope your family is all right.' My brain started working again. This morning, Dad had talked about going to Fazazz. He was excited about some classic car they had. He'd joked about buying Mum a model car kit for her birthday. Today was my mother's birthday. I wanted to howl. I wanted to find her and Dad. I wanted Blake to text saying he was okay.

An image of Fazazz flashed in my mind. The showroom – on the bottom floor of an old building. It'd be okay, it had survived the September quake.

But it might not be okay. All the buildings now in ruins around me had survived September. I wanted to go and see for myself if my father was in that shop drooling over an ancient car. He'd be helping anyone who was hurt, if only I knew where. He was calm in a crisis. He made you believe things would be all right.

People everywhere, all walking away, intent on leaving the broken city. They looked shocked and dazed. I couldn't look up, not after I saw a guy frantically waving his shirt out a fourth-storey window.

I edged past a pile of masonry. Men in high-vis vests clambered over it. I wanted to help too. Mum and Dad would be helping. Blake could be too. But what if…

I kept walking.

At the corner, I stopped. Which way now? To my right, the mall section of Cashel Street was a disaster. Gaping holes in the buildings. Windows gone. Bricks and masonry lying shattered on the street. People searching, helping others escape through gaps in walls. My eyes skipped over a shape on the ground, covered by a couple of towels. Just beyond it, people clambered over a heap of rubble.

'Mum?' A chunk of something heavy fell from a building just ahead. I hurried, going faster where the buildings were higher. 'Mum!' It was her. She was up on the pile of bricks and concrete, clearing a path to the wrecked shop behind, her face intent.

A man with a helmet and orange vest said, 'This is no place for you, kid. You need to get home. Off you go.'

'That's my mum. I have to tell her I'm all right. I have to find out where Dad is.' I couldn't take my eyes off her.

'I'll get her. But then you scarper. Deal?'

I nodded. 'Thanks.'

The man called out, 'Clemmie!' She lifted her head to look at him. He pointed at me.

I saw her lips form my name. *'Lyla!'* She picked her way down the rubble heap. Her feet were bare.

Her arms around me were bliss. 'Lyla. Darling. You're all right?' She held me at arm's length. *'Is that your blood?'*

I kept my grip on her hand. 'No. Tell you later. Where's Dad? Blake? Have you heard anything?'

She shook her head. 'Nothing. It'll take hours for texts to come through.' She looked away from me – but

I'd already seen her tears. 'It's terrible. Go home, Lyla. Keep safe. Please?'

I didn't want to go home. I wanted to stay, to help. Another rule from after September thrummed in my brain: *obey instructions.* I fought not to argue. She didn't need that. 'Okay. You stay safe, Mum.' I tried not to imagine the buildings around us tumbling down on her and the other rescuers.

'Good girl.' Another hug and she turned from me.

'Mum! Wait.' I tugged my shoes off. Shoes – not sandals. It had been cold this morning. I pushed them into her hands. 'Put them on. Don't argue – please. I want to help. It'll help you to wear these.'

She brushed her feet clear of dirt and grit before she put them on. 'Thanks, love. They'll help a lot. Be careful, won't you? There's glass everywhere.' Then she was off, back to the work of clearing a way to get into the building. I couldn't remember what it had been before it fell into a pile of nothing.

I left my white socks on my feet. One of Mum's high-heeled sandals lay in the middle of the street.

I swallowed a sob. *Dad, please be alive.*

I walked away from the city centre, one of hundreds, all of us with our shocked faces, some of us covered in dust and blood. Several people asked me if I was okay. A lot of Ian's blood had got onto the white hotel robe. I hoped he was in hospital by now. I hoped he hadn't… *don't go there.*

Sirens shrieked and the sky vibrated with the throb of helicopters.

Where was Dad? *Don't think about piles of masonry, scattered bricks.*

I walked, all the time checking anyone caring for the injured. I passed a couple of makeshift triage areas, but Dad wasn't at either of them.

High-vis vests were everywhere. I'd thought we were done with them by now. They'd been all over the city in the months after the September quake, along with the men in hard hats driving cranes and diggers. There hadn't been a street in the city without orange road cones. Now they were back. The road I walked on was split and buckled, great rifts torn in the seal.

It took me ages to get home. There were so many people, so many cars crawling along choked roads whose signs had either gone or pointed the wrong way. I walked through a city I didn't recognise, its familiar landmarks pulverised. A tree Blake and I had climbed when we were small lay on the ground, its roots sticking up.

I came to a street that was open. I couldn't think of its name. I joined the mass of people, all of us walking in the middle. Cars and pedestrians mixed together on the shattered road.

On every road leading out of the city, cars were nose to tail. They bounced up and down whenever another shock hit. So many cars. It would be quicker to walk.

Grey muddy eruptions spurted up through cracks. I dodged around the ones I could until a woman touched my arm. 'It's just liquefaction. The quake's turned the ground to mush, just like last time.'

I should have worked that out for myself but I'd only seen it then when it was like lakes spread all over the ground.

I saw a convoy of huge cranes heading into the central city. I wouldn't let myself think about why they were needed.

Puddles of grey liquefaction stretched right across the roads. I abandoned my socks after I'd waded through the first one.

The danger of high buildings falling faded as I reached the suburbs. Now the danger was of stepping into a deep hole hidden by the horrible liquefaction.

I walked past houses shoved off their foundations. Past people sitting outside, too stunned to move, too frightened to go into their wrecked homes.

As I drew nearer Ireland Street, I sped up. Our house would be all right. It had survived September. It would be fine. I slowed down again. The turning into Ireland Street was just ahead. What if…

A woman ran past me, looked around frantically, then clambered over a collapsed stone wall and started sloshing through liquefaction towards the house, shouting, 'Roger! Where are you? Oh, I knew I shouldn't have left you all by yourself!'

She'd left a kid at home by himself?

'Can I help?' I started picking my way through the sticky mess.

She gave a sob. 'He's so little. My husband said he needed to get used to being outside and now he could be dead. Roger! Come on, darling. Mumma's home.'

This wasn't making any sense. 'Um, how old is he? Has he got a favourite hiding place?'

She stared at me as if I was the crazy one. 'I told you – today's the first day he's been outside.' She started squelching towards the back of the house.

I yelled, 'What's he look like? Can he walk?'

She didn't even turn around. 'Of all the stupid questions! Did you ever meet a puppy that couldn't walk?'

'Well,' I muttered, 'it's pretty stupid to expect me to know Roger's a dog.'

She heard me and came sploshing back. 'I'm so sorry. I'm just so worried. Roger! Tell Mumma where you are!'

'Listen!' I waded closer to the house. 'I think he's under the deck.'

She just about fell headlong into the liquefaction, she was in such a hurry. 'Roger darling, it's all right. Come out now. Come to Mumma.'

I bent down to look under the deck. All I could see was his head and his terrified eyes – he was up to his belly in gunk. He whimpered when he saw me. 'Hang on, Roger. We'll soon have you out of there.'

Mumma just stood there, wringing her hands. I had to shout at her to get her to listen. 'Have you got an axe? Or a crowbar? Something we can use to take boards off?'

That got her attention. 'We can't do that! The house isn't damaged. We can't just start ripping it up!'

I couldn't be bothered arguing. It seemed that shock took people in different ways. Selina from the square became calm. Ian was polite even though he might have been dying. I felt better if I could do something. So I took off the bathrobe and crawled under the deck. Liquefaction up to my elbows, halfway up my thighs.

'Hey, Roger. It's okay, buddy. You're in a bit of a fix there, old fella.'

There can't be many things as sad as a puppy stuck in liquefaction. Roger didn't take his eyes off me as I crawled towards him. I reached out to give him a tug, but my hand got the most slobbery licking ever. 'Okay! You're pleased to see me. I get it!'

I had to get both hands under him to haul him free. He rewarded me by washing my entire face with his tongue. Oh well, one way to get a clean face.

I wriggled backwards with him in my arms. Mumma seized him, mud and all, smothering the un-gunky bits of him with kisses. Roger might be a terrier, and very possibly his coat might be white. Bits of it, anyway.

I sat on her steps, clear of the mud. 'Can I have something to wipe this stuff off?' No point asking for water. We'd been without water for days after the September quake, and this one had to be worse.

She stared at me, horrified. 'But I'll leave mud on the floor if I go inside!'

I'd had enough of her. 'Fine.'

I got to my feet, but she thrust Roger into my arms. 'Sorry! I don't know what's wrong with me. Wait here. Please.'

I sat down again and Roger and I had a good chat. I swear he smiled at me. 'You're quite sweet, you are,' I told him. He needed a good clean-up too.

Mumma came back with a pink towel. 'It's one of my best ones. You deserve the best.'

I choked up, but shook my head. 'S'okay. I'm glad we found him.'

I cleaned the stinking muck from my arms and legs as well as I could and put the bathrobe back on, glad of its warmth even though by now it was an artistic mess of blood and mud.

Mumma came out to the road to say goodbye, holding Roger in her arms. I gave him a rub under his chin. 'Bye, old fella.'

They were still watching when I got to my corner. Roger gave a yipping bark when I waved.

There was liquefaction in our street too, great lakes of the evil stuff.

A whole entire corner of the Jaffries' house had gone, exposing the lounge. Nothing was left on the walls. Liquefaction covered the lawn. The foundations of the Chans' house had been punched up about half a metre on one side right under the two youngest kids' bedroom. The house looked okay except it was on a wicked tilt.

Nobody home in either place that I could see. I hoped I wasn't the only one here right now. I couldn't stand not knowing if we still had a home, or if it was just a pile of sticks.

I began running.

I sprinted through the sludge, forgetting to be careful of holes, turned the corner. We still had a house. The walls were upright. The roof looked okay. Blake's bedroom window had a jagged hole, but apart from that it seemed fine.

I didn't have my key. It was in my backpack and I hadn't remembered to pick it up after I'd taken it off to help Ian in Cathedral Square.

There was a spare one stashed in a fake rock by the garage, but the garage had taken a massive sideways hit and there was no sign of the rock.

A big crack ran the length of the step into the house. I eased myself down onto it. I didn't want to go inside. I didn't want to see the mess the earthquake had left us. I didn't want to be by myself.

I checked my phone. No messages from Dad or Blake. My head sank to my knees. My legs were filthy. My feet stung. The earth shook.

I should go and check on the neighbours. Five minutes. I'd go in five minutes. I just needed to stop shivering.

'Lyla! You okay?'

It was Blake, dirty like I was, worried like I was. I threw myself at him and for the first time in years we hugged, holding each other tight.

'The parents?' he asked, still keeping hold of me. 'You heard anything?'

'Mum. She was rescuing people in Cashel Street. Haven't heard from Dad.'

His arms fell away from me. 'Me neither.' He pulled out his key. 'Your mates? And Greer?'

'Katie and Shona were okay. They were going straight home. Not sure about Greer. Shona didn't know where she'd be.' I pulled the robe tight around me. 'Were you at uni when it happened? Are people okay?'

Blake nodded. 'There's only a bit of damage from what I could see. Didn't hear of any casualties.' He put the key in the lock. 'You ready for this?'

'Yeah. It's cold out here.' There'd be no way of getting warm inside, though. We'd had to wait a few days in September before water and electricity worked again.

It took both of us to wrestle the door open. The entrance hall didn't look too bad, although the bookcase had shed its five shelves of books, just like last time. The mirror was on the floor with a wide crack running across its back. We stepped over everything.

In the lounge the TV lay facedown among the DVDs. Pictures hung askew, but at least they'd stayed on the walls. The nest of small tables lay on a pile of Dad's car magazines. 'Blake – Dad was going to Fazazz. It might have collapsed. He might…' I gulped.

He stepped over Mum's beloved house plants lying in a mess of spilled dirt on the carpet. 'Nah. It was nearly one o'clock when the quake hit. He'd have been on his way to meet Mum for lunch. You know where they were going?'

I shook my head. We should have asked.

Blake gave my back a pat crossed with a bash. 'Come on. Nothing we can do about the parents except wait for them to turn up. Bet they will, too.' He headed for the kitchen and stopped, shaking his head. 'September all over again.' He booted the dishwasher door shut.

He was right, damn it. It was stupid to worry. It didn't make anything different. I kicked stuff out of my way – rice, flour, sugar, pasta, something red – paprika?

Chilli powder? A bottle leaked oil into a spill of yellow mustard.

'Watch it, Lyla! That stuff's full of busted china.'

I picked my way to the sink, turned the tap on. Nothing. September all over again with the water situation too. The emergency water container was intact. We each downed a glass of water – and jumped through the roof when the landline rang. It was a plug-into-the-wall job with the handset attached to a cord and it worked without electricity or internet. Dad – and heaps of other Christchurch people – had bought one after September.

It was Dad's parents ringing now, all the way from the Sunshine Coast. Blake grabbed it first. 'Oh hi, Nana Lilith. Yeah, it's big. No. Just me and Lyla. Mum's okay – well, she was when Lyla saw her just after. Haven't heard from Dad.'

A squawking panic erupted from the receiver. My brother rolled his eyes at me. 'Yeah, we'll call you. But listen, Nana – you know what Dad's like. He'll be right in there helping people.'

He'd only just put the phone down when it rang again. The Wellington grands this time. 'Mum's okay. Lyla talked to her just after… No. But the phones are jammed… Lucky you hadn't taken off. Yeah, we will.'

He hung up. 'Dad's going to be fine, Lyla. They'll be home at some stage, both of them.'

I swallowed a hard knot of fear. 'I know. I just wish…'

He gave my back another brotherly swipe. 'Yeah. Me too.'

Five

The idiot quakes were so random – one house in a street could be almost undamaged and everything else unliveable. It looked like this time we were the lucky ones – at least we could live in ours.

I bent to start putting things back, but Blake stopped me. 'First things first, Lyla. We'll check on the neighbours. All this can wait. It's not going anywhere.'

Oh. Yeah, of course. My brain seemed to have seized up. Not good, Lyla. Time to get with the program.

We divided Ireland Street between us. I'd do Natalie's house next door. Next on my list was Mrs Malone, then the Prof. Then, oh joy, tucked in the curve of the cul-de-sac, was Matt Nagel's place. A catalogue of Matt's past sins was vivid in my memory – the way he'd hide to jump out at me on dark winter evenings, pelt me with rotten fruit in autumn, let down my bike tyres. All those things still made me spitting mad… I shook my head. Suck it up, Lyla. There were people in town risking their lives right now. I could take Mr Thinks-he's-so-smart Nagel.

I jabbed at my phone yet again just in case I'd somehow missed a text from Dad.

'Leave it, Lyla. You'll flatten the battery.'

I'd forgotten. We had no electricity to charge phones. 'Come on. If we're going to do this we'd better get started.'

'We need gumboots,' Blake said.

We both stared down at our filthy legs. I shrugged. 'No point.'

'Enjoy wading through liquefaction and sewage, do you?'

I hated it when he came over all big-brother-ish, and I hated it more when he was right. I picked my way across the passage to the laundry. Chaos reigned. I had to excavate the boots from under a heap of clothes, washing powder, brooms and mops. The washing machine had again migrated across the floor, and the dryer hung askew on the wall. I grabbed our parents' boots while I was at it.

I staggered back to the kitchen, laden with eight boots. Blake had retrieved a packet of wipes from the mess. He wasn't as mucky as I was, but between us we used up the whole packet.

He said, 'You realise we'll need to resurrect the long-drop too.'

I screwed up my face. 'Crap. The long-drop situation all over again.' Also known as the trek out to the far corner of the backyard to answer calls of nature.

He patted my head. 'Don't worry, sis. It's a man's job.'

Usually, a statement like that would make me explode all over him – not this time. He was welcome to dig out the stinky hole.

We didn't bother trying to wrestle the door shut when we left the house.

Natalie and the boys weren't home, but they'd probably be able to live in their house – it looked in about the same state as ours from what I could see on the outside. The back door gaped open. Inside, there was the same old shambles we had. I retrieved the notepad she kept by the phone from the clutter on the floor and tore a page from it. *Come to ours. Lyla.*

I took the pen and notepad with me and waded towards the two houses at the end of the cul-de-sac. The ground was lower here and both places were swimming in liquefaction. All I could see of Mrs Malone's garden was the tops of red flowers drooping into the gunk. It was going to break her heart. I waded up the path. It wasn't easy – broken concrete tilted every which way. I hoped she wasn't home and injured, or… If she was okay she'd be out with a shovel, swearing and digging. It wasn't fair to wreck an eighty-two-year-old's garden.

I was glad of my gummies as I tested each step to make sure I wasn't going to fall neck-deep into a stinking sinkhole. The front wall of the house leant out at a crazy angle. I made my way round the back. The door was locked. I pounded on it. 'Mrs Malone! Are you okay?'

No reply. Just as I was wondering whether it'd be a good idea to kick in a window and climb through it, a voice called from the house next door – the one equally drowning in foul stuff.

'Don't worry, Lyla. She's at her grandson's. I met them just now on my way home.' There was a cackle of laughter. 'She was spitting tacks.'

I slopped across to the fence. 'What about you, Prof? You've got a bit of a situation too.' Prof was old too – older than Mrs Malone, or so she reckoned.

'As you see, I'm still alive.' He frowned at the lake in his backyard. 'I should have specialised in geology instead of mathematics. A geologist would have thought about the ground under his house.'

'Go to ours. We'll boil up water for tea when we're done with checking on people.'

His eyes lit up. 'I'll be right there. Don't worry about the Jaffrie or Chan places – I checked them just now.'

I handed him the pen and paper. 'Can you leave notes? Tell them to come to ours. The quake hasn't busted our place too badly except for the garage.'

I wished the Prof had had time to check on the Nagels' place too. I dithered on the front steps – Matt might look like every girl's dream with his blond hair and built body but he was so not my favourite fifteen-year-old male. *Oh, just get it over with, Lyla Sherwin.* I called out the usual, 'Anyone home?'

I got a response – a groan and a string of swearing.

So Matt Nagel was still alive. 'Okay! I'm coming in.'

The front door was locked, or maybe stuck – didn't matter anyway, not with its glass panel cracked to glory. I booted it till it shattered.

I scrambled over everything on the hall floor, following the sound of his voice, then came to a dead stop in the lounge doorway. I could only see half of Matt's body. His left side from shoulder down to foot lay squashed under what used to be the outside wall. It looked like some of the upper storey was on him as well.

He groaned, then muttered, 'You took your time.'

I jumped across the rubbish on the floor, my mind spinning. How could I get him free? I wouldn't be able to lift that stuff. 'I'll get Blake. We need two of us.'

He grabbed my ankle with his right hand. 'No! Just get me out of here.'

I heard his desperation, but still I hesitated – there was so much rubble, and it looked heavy.

'Please, Lyla.'

It was the *please* that clinched it. Matt Nagel had never before used that word around me. I began hauling chunks of timber and plaster from the load pinning him down, working carefully. It was like playing Jenga or pick-up-sticks, except the price of losing was unthinkable.

His face was screwed up with pain and every now and then he'd give a sort of grunt.

The top layer of rubbish wasn't too heavy, but it had been hiding the heavy beam that had crashed down on him and crushed a little table that somehow seemed to be taking some of the weight – lucky for him. I tugged at the beam. Couldn't budge it. 'I'll have to get Blake.'

Matt's eyes shot open. 'Use a lever.'

Give me a lever and I'll move the world. Somebody had said that or something like it a millennia or two ago. I dragged a wooden dining chair across the floor, bumping it over the rubbish. Sliding the back under the beam, I jammed a chunk of wood under it to act as a pivot, then stood on the legs. The beam lifted slightly.

It wasn't enough – there still wasn't a gap between Matt and the beam – but he was wriggling and grimacing, and after long, shaking minutes the top half of him was free.

His leg was still stuck. Even with all my weight on the chair the beam only shifted a fraction. 'It won't lift any higher. Can you sit up? It might change the angle or something.'

Matt was groaning, the building was groaning and it felt like the chair was going to crack.

Hurry.

It seemed to take ages for him to sit up. I wanted to lean over to help, but everything felt too precarious and I was terrified that even a small movement would crash the beam back on to his shin and foot.

Finally he was upright. He put his right hand under his left knee and with a mix of wriggling and tugging got his leg out from under the crushing weight then slumped forward, his good arm around his good knee.

I stepped off the chair and stood for a moment, hands over my face while I tried to stop shaking. So close – if that beam had fallen just a few centimetres further in...

The shape under the towels in the city surfaced in my mind. I shut it down. *Matt's okay. Concentrate on that.* 'Water?'

'Kitchen. Under sink.'

Same old quake mess in their kitchen, plus the dishwasher had come open and sicked everything up across the floor. The china was the sort that shatters like glass. I found the emergency water supply and the plastic beaker beside it.

Matt had scooted away from the crumbled wall and was leaning against a chair cradling his left arm when I came back. I looked at the wreckage of the room rather than at the tear tracks down his face. 'Your mum's not going to be happy.' The whole wall was practically gone and a good section of the top storey was lying splayed out on the back lawn.

He grunted, which I took to mean that I'd just uttered the understatement of the century.

'Let's get out of here.' I was acutely aware of the rocking, rolling floor and the creaking of timber.

Matt held out his right hand. I hauled on it and helped him stand, but when he tried to put weight on his left foot he almost fell back down. His mother wasn't going to be happy with his injuries, either. If she could wrap him in bubble wrap forever, she'd do it.

We managed to get outside the house, although he nearly crushed me to death when I had to take his weight. 'I'm getting Blake.' I didn't give Matt time to object – too bad if he didn't like it.

Even with Blake's help, it was a mission to get Matt across to our place. He was heavy, and with Blake being taller than me, I got most of the weight. We made a seat with our hands to carry him over the liquefaction. He objected. 'A bit of sludge isn't going to hurt me.'

'It'll hurt us because you'll stink,' I said.

'And Lyla's used up all the wipes,' my brother said. 'Quit arguing and obey instructions.'

Wow! That worked. Still, it seemed ages before we could dump him on the sofa back at ours.

Prof was there, busy with a broom and rubbish bag clearing the kitchen mess. He dropped everything after one glance at Matt. 'Let's take a look at those injuries, young man. Lyla, can you find scissors? We'll need to cut those jeans off.'

Matt lifted his right hand by way of reply. His eyes were screwed shut, his mouth much the same. I located the kitchen scissors and Prof snipped the jeans just below the knee. 'Nasty graze on that shin,' he said. The ankle was worse. It was swollen, grazed, gashed and bleeding.

Blake saw the blood and plopped to the floor, his face a pale shade of green.

'I'm okay,' Matt muttered.

He clearly wasn't, and the big question was: just how not-okay was he? How were we supposed to deal with the Matt situation? If only Dad was home. Things were never so bad when he was there.

But I didn't even know if my father was still alive.

I breathed in. Out. In again. Blake was useless with bloody injuries. Prof said, 'We need to get you to a doctor, young man.'

Matt gave him a slight grin. 'Think you can piggy-back me, Prof? I'm okay.'

Prof frowned, but Matt was right – right about not being able to get to a doctor, that is, not right about the okay bit. I said, 'Can you move your foot? Wriggle your toes?'

Matt opened his eyes enough to glare at me. 'Shut it, Lyla. Nothing's broken. I know what broken bones feel like. It's just bruising, that's all.'

'I'll get ice,' Blake said.

Matt grumbled something about making a fuss but he didn't object when Blake dumped a bag of still-frozen peas across his ankle. He didn't say anything either when I used some of our precious water supply to clean his wounds. Prof raided Dad's first-aid box for antiseptic ointment and bandages. We did all we could for our patient, but he didn't seem very grateful. I gave him painkillers. That earned me a grunt.

Blake boiled water for tea on our emergency camp cooker. Prof helped me search the kitchen chaos for something to drink from. 'Two plastic mugs!' He waved them like they were trophies.

I flourished my own finds. 'A soup bowl and a mug. China, both of them.' I wished I could make Matt drink from the soup bowl, but that would be too mean seeing he could only use one hand. He'd have done it to me, though. Lucky for him I was so nice.

Blake handed him the china mug. 'Your house is totally munted, mate.'

Matt nodded. 'The olds are going to be pretty gutted when they see the damage. They went to Oamaru. Meant to be staying the night but they're probably on their way back by now.'

'You didn't go to school today.' I didn't rub it in that if he had gone to school then he wouldn't have been at home when the quake hit.

'No point. No PE.'

The Prof brought his plastic mug of tea over and perched himself beside Matt on the sofa. I thought he was going to come out with a lecture about how subjects like English and Maths could help with a sports career, but no. 'Let's take a look at that shoulder, Matt. I'm not convinced that it's just bad bruising. Crush injuries can be serious.'

'It's just bruising. Not even any blood.' Man, he was snappy.

Prof got stern. 'Off with that shirt, young man.'

'Yep,' I said, 'black and blue already.' A slight exaggeration, but I could sure see where his skin was getting up a good rainbow of colours.

Prof helped Matt button his shirt. 'It looks like you'll live. But tell us if you notice any sharp pains or localised swelling.'

I longed for word from Dad, but there was still nothing on my phone. When the landline rang, I jumped for it, just beating Blake to pick it up. 'Dad?'

It wasn't Dad – of course it wouldn't be. It was Matt's mother. 'Lyla, at last! I've been ringing and ringing everyone I can think of. Where's Matthew? You're at home so you must have seen him. Where is he? Why haven't you called me? You must know I'd be worried sick.'

How come she thought I had her number? I didn't even try to interrupt. Matt was welcome to her. Without saying anything, I unplugged the phone from the wall, took it into the lounge and plugged it into the jack. I let it ring twice. 'Mrs Nagel? What happened? Hang on, I'll get Matt for you.'

The cord wasn't long enough to reach him. I put it on speaker and he leant sideways. 'Cool it, Mum.'

He winced as she exploded. Blake, Prof and I all heard every word she shrieked at him. 'Matthew! Darling, are you all right? I've been frantic! I thought you'd been killed.'

'Chill, Mum. I'm fine. Not a scratch on me. Can't say the same for the house, though…'

'We'll come and get you. We'll leave right now. I knew in my bones we shouldn't have left you alone today. Fiona and Jed say we can stay down here with them. Oamaru's safe.'

Matt shut his eyes, took a huge breath and said, 'Mum, put Dad on, will you?'

We heard a bit of a tussle at the other end, then Mr Nagel's voice. 'Matt? What's the state of play?'

According to Matt's side of the conversation, the house was a wreck (true) and he was fine except for twisting his ankle on a loose piece of concrete on his way home from school. 'Stay in Oamaru, Dad. I can camp at the Sherwins'.' He nodded at me to hang up the receiver and slumped back looking exhausted.

Six

I wasn't especially hungry even though I hadn't had any lunch – shock, I guess. But I needed distraction, to keep busy. 'Blake, let's put the barbie on the back porch. Can you get it going? I'll raid the freezer.'

The voice from the sofa said, 'Gas bottles at mine if yours run out. In the garage.'

At least Matt's brain was functioning, or it might just have been his stomach reacting to the promise of food.

The chest freezer was in the laundry, the same small room where the dryer dangled from the wall and the washing machine had danced across the floor. Going in there felt like diving into dangerous water. I held my breath and scrabbled around grabbing packets of pizza, sausages and a couple of loaves of bread. The sensible part of me fully knew that holding my breath wasn't going to stop the dryer from crashing off the wall, but the scared part needed all the help it could get.

Blake could do the cooking. Barbecuing and long-drop digging were both definitely man jobs. Apparently

Prof thought so too, because both of them disappeared outside.

Matt shifted on the sofa, doing a lot of face-pulling in the process.

'Are you okay?'

He shrugged his good shoulder. 'Is there a radio we can listen to? It's got to be bad in town.'

I wasn't sure I wanted to listen, but I found the battery radio and gave it to him. Maybe he saw something in my face, because he said, 'You were in town? It's bad?'

'Worse than bad.' I turned away. Mum and Dad were somewhere in that chaos.

He switched the radio on. It was four o'clock, and a news bulletin was just starting. Words dropped like lead weights into the room. *Multiple fatalities, extensive damage, trapped people, destruction, fire, chaos, emergency services*, a woman saying *I was so frightened.*

I couldn't listen. I got up from my chair, and *wham*, the whole house slammed sideways. I dropped to the floor, hands over my head. Matt yelled, 'Freaking aftershocks!'

The announcer kept on reading the news in his calm, concerned voice. I huddled on the floor, listening to Matt cursing. A huge crash came from the laundry.

'What the...' Matt shouted.

'It'll be the dryer.' I eased myself up to sitting. I was in that room not even five minutes ago. *Stay safe.* I shouldn't have gone in there. I shouldn't have taken such a stupid risk. I sat with my head in my hands shaking with my own private earthquake.

'Stuff this,' Matt said. 'Being in the middle of news as it happens sucks.'

'You should go to Oamaru.'

'Be my guest.'

And stay with his crazy mother? Staying here with the crazy earth was the better option. My mind skipped to the city. This would have shaken more loose pieces to the ground there too. I hoped somebody had given Mum a hard hat.

There was a thumping on the front door. 'Lyla? The door's stuck.'

Natalie and her boys. Life went on, if you were lucky – and I'd probably just used up my life's quota of luck.

I tottered to the door. We got it open between us, and they fell inside, shocked, chilled and grubby.

'Stay here for a sec. We'll clean you up a bit.' I ran to the linen cupboard and fought to open those doors too – and when I did all the towels fell out.

I grabbed three and kicked the rest back. The doors didn't shut properly. The whole house must be on a lean.

I helped Natalie clean the gunk off the boys' legs. 'You walked home?'

She nodded. 'The car's still in town. I parked it beside a brick wall.'

I stared at her. 'Will you, uh...get it back when the roads are fixed?' It wasn't what I wanted to say. Was it flattened? Had she nearly been killed? Had she seen Dad? But there were her boys, both of them looking lost and terrified.

'It's in town and there's a cordon up. Nobody's allowed in.'

I reached out for Henry and Leo. 'Come on, men. How does a hot chocolate sound?'

They let me lead them into the lounge. I parked them together in a squashy chair and tucked a blanket around them. 'Sit down, Natalie. I'll get drinks all round. Matt, what do you want? And don't say beer.'

I made coffee on the camp stove for him and Natalie, chocolate for me and the boys. Blake and Prof came in from the barbecue carrying a plate of pizza. It was scorched on the bottom and still a bit chilly on top.

The two little boys shook their heads and Natalie looked ready to cry. I took a slice and waved it at them. 'Watch this, guys. This is the proper way to eat pizza.' I held the sharp end and took a bite from the crust.

Matt took a slice, heaving a dramatic sigh. 'Girls! They haven't got a clue. This is how you do proper pizza-eating.' He chomped off a huge bite from halfway down.

Leo giggled and reached for a slice. After a moment, Henry did the same. 'No, *this* is the proper way,' Leo said.

Natalie turned to mouth *thank you* at the pair of us.

It's amazing what you can find to say about pizza when you want to distract a couple of terrified kids. Prof talked about how there was no pizza around when he was their age. Blake insisted the only correct topping was pineapple, salami and prawns.

But all good things come to an end, apparently, and when Natalie was finished she said, 'Lyla, I need to see what's happening at work. They'll probably have set up something to treat people but the computers won't be working. It'll be chaotic.'

I did not want to be responsible for two traumatised kids who right now had tears washing down their faces all over again at the idea of their mother leaving. But I wanted to be useful, and making it possible for Natalie to get to the medical centre was useful. I'd seen her at work, cheerful and welcoming behind the reception desk and probably holding the whole place together. 'Don't worry.' I squeezed myself into the chair between them. 'There's a lot to do around here and these two are expert helpers.'

Natalie's tense shoulders slumped with relief. 'You're a gem. I don't want to go, but...'

'It's okay. Come back here when you're done. You can all sleep here if you want. It'll be good to have company.'

Natalie hugged her boys. 'Will you help Lyla? She won't know where to find the duvets in our house.'

They stared at her with huge eyes. Henry whimpered, 'Stay here, Mummy.'

She crouched in front of them. 'I'll come back, I promise. The doctors and nurses need me to help them with the hurt people.'

'Matt's hurt,' Leo said.

Matt dropped his voice to a thrilling whisper. 'Hey, guys – when your mum's gone, do you wanna see my bruises?'

It turned out that it didn't matter if a boy was six, eight or fifteen – war wounds were up there with tomato sauce and barbecued sausages. I was still shaking my head at the sight of the three of them trying to decide where each bruise ended and another started when there was more hammering on the door.

I wrenched the door open and Cindy Jaffrie tumbled through.

She gasped out, 'Caroline? Alex? Are they here?'

'No…'

She collapsed to the floor before I could say anything else, but what could I say? *They'll be okay* wouldn't be any use.

I crouched down. 'Shush, please, Cindy! Natalie's boys are here and they're freaked out already.'

'Sorry.'

I watched her shut the panic back in its box. She got up. 'Okay. I'm okay now.' Neither of us mentioned her shattered house.

I gave her arm a squeeze. 'Come on, let's get that mud off you.' I got her a towel, then went for more when the Chan family fell through the door a minute late – Marlene, Robert and their three small girls. 'I found your note and it was all smudged but Mummy said we'd come here because our house is very, very sad,' Imelda, the seven-year-old, said, looking very, very sad herself.

Mum would still be working in the city. She'd be cold.

Dad, where are you?

Seven

I went outside to bring in sausages and bread warmed from frozen on the barbie. I edged up to Blake. 'It's after eight. It'll be dark soon. We should have heard from Dad by now. Do you think…'

Prof answered, his hand on my shoulder. 'He'll be flat out, Lyla. They'll be needing every medical person they can find.'

Blake, his eyes firmly on the sizzling sausages, said, 'Network's still jammed. He'll be okay, sis. Here, take these.'

It was stupid to worry, except how were you meant not to? I took the dish of sausages, sauce and bread into the lounge.

Leo and Henry ate sausages without noticing what they were doing – they were too busy giggling at Matt eating his by taking alternate bites from the ends.

'Disgusting!' Imelda Chan rolled her eyes and ate hers in small, dainty bites.

We kept the radio low enough not to bother the kids. The news from town was bad. The multistorey CTV building was burning, and people were still in there. Cindy Jaffrie went dead white. Marlene Chan grabbed her. 'Caroline doesn't work in that building, Cindy. She'll be all right. Town's a shattered mess. It'll take her ages to get home.'

Caroline Jaffrie, Alex Jaffrie, Dad. Mum. We had to believe the four of them would be all right. I hoped Greer would be too. Their house had been deep in liquefaction in September. If it was like that again they wouldn't be able to stay in it until it was cleared.

Katie's house had a landline. Duh! I ran for the phone. Oh God, I hoped she was all right – she hadn't rung me either.

There was no reply. I set the receiver down carefully. What did no reply mean? Surely both she and Shona had got home safely from town. Surely.

I had to keep busy or go mad. I made more tea and hot chocolate. Leo looked up at me, his eyes full of shadows no eight-year-old should have. 'Lyla, guess where I was?'

'When the earth went crazy?' I grinned at him – capable, un-scare-able Lyla. 'Up a tree? No? Okay, how about in the toilet?'

Tears overflowed. 'I was scared.'

I bent down to his level and in my best dramatic whisper, said, 'Did your wee go all over the floor?'

Henry giggled and, after a moment, Leo said, 'Everywhere! And I didn't care either.'

I gave him a hug, then squashed Henry into my arms as well. 'Awesome, dude!'

Cindy Jaffrie looked wrung out. She squeezed in beside Prof at the end of Matt's sofa. He nodded at the mug teetering in her hand. 'Drink that tea, my dear. It'll do you good.'

It was a long, long evening. In some weird, out-of-this-world kind of way it was good – neighbours, all of us together helping each other. But then I'd think about Dad, Mum, Katie, Shona, Greer, Joanne. Images from the devastation in the city crashed in over the top and I'd have to concentrate really hard on something else.

Who knew you could cook frozen pizza on a barbecue? Sausages were nicer, though, and it was good to have half-frozen bread to wrap them in – the bread thawed and cooled the sausage at the same time.

People made the trek out to the long-drop. Robert Chan took the little boys out. He and Blake helped Matt outside too, although I'd be willing to bet a large fortune that they only went as far as the nearest bush.

I didn't want to believe the radio reports were about our city. They were saying people were dead. Others were injured. The rescue helicopter was using the road outside the hospital's emergency department as a landing pad. The hospital put out a call asking off-duty staff to come in if they possibly could.

Dad could have gone to help at the hospital.

Daylight was fading. Henry snuggled up against me. 'I don't like the dark.'

Leo didn't say anything, and I knew he was trying desperately not to let the tears out. I wrapped my arms around both of them. 'You reckon it's time to get the emergency lights?'

Henry took the thumb from his mouth to nod. Leo said, 'We won't be able to find them if it gets dark first.'

'Good thinking.' We did the high five. 'And what do you reckon about everybody sleeping in here tonight? I'll organise the lights and you two organise people to drag all the mattresses in here. Can you do that?'

They jumped up, and went to try to drag Matt off the sofa.

'Blake – the emergency lights. They're in the garage.' The munted, busted, shoved-off-its-foundations garage.

Robert Chan stood up. 'Come on, Blake. Let's see if we can get in.'

I said, 'Hey guys, leave Matt – he's too lazy to be any use. But we're the awesome mattress-finders.'

Henry scampered down the hall, jumping over broken pictures and the heap from the linen cupboard. He stopped at my doorway. 'Your room's wrecked, Lyla.'

I wanted to cry but Leo was beside me, quivering with stress, so I swore instead. The kids stared at me open mouthed, then collapsed into giggles. But it wasn't damn well funny – the dressing table was still fixed to the wall but it had spat every single drawer out across the room. The whole place was a merry old mess of clothes and broken glass from the mirror. The noticeboard was on the floor and my bedside light lay squashed under the tipped-over desk.

Leo took my hand. 'It's all right, Lyla. We'll help you.'

Ouch. He was only eight, and totally freaked out, but was comforting me. I gave him a hug. 'Good man. Let's do it.'

They helped me kick a path to the bed and between us we wrestled the mattress off. I'd have done it a lot quicker by myself, and we'd only got as far as the lounge door by the time Blake and Robert came back with the lanterns. The light made puddles in the gloom. Light puddles were friendlier than liquefaction puddles.

'We've got mattresses at our house,' Leo said.

Not a bad idea – but I let the men haul them over from next door. Our house was now a meeting house, a real wharenui – wall-to-wall mattresses on the lounge floor, marae style.

Henry and Leo fell asleep and the Chan girls shortly after, although Imelda took her time. We turned the radio on low enough not to disturb them.

We heard shock in people's voices, grief in their words.

Somebody official said people shouldn't expect help to reach the suburbs for at least three days.

Voices kept saying people had died but nobody could confirm how many. Cindy Jaffrie breathed in short gasps. Marlene held her hand. None of us tried to tell her that her daughter and husband would be okay.

We put a lantern in the lounge window where the light would be visible from the street.

It was fully dark and raining when we heard somebody struggling with the door. Cindy just beat me and Blake to get to it. Caroline Jaffrie fell in.

Cindy hugged her daughter as if she'd never let her go. Blake shoved an assortment of food at her – pizza, sausage and a plate of soft ice-cream. The stuff would be melting in freezers all over the city.

Cindy wrapped a blanket around Caroline, questions pouring out. 'Your father's building, Caroline. Is it… Did you see him? Is he okay?'

Caroline shook her head. 'Don't know. I couldn't find him – one entire wall's down. The building's a shambles but it looks like they all got out.'

She'd walked home. They weren't letting people into the parking building. Her car was stuck there.

It was good Caroline was here and safe, but I couldn't help wishing it was Dad who'd come through the door.

I hoped my parents wouldn't have to walk home; they'd taken the car this morning. They could have parked it on the street. My mind skipped to the image of Mum clambering over the pile of rubble. *Please, let her be all right. Let them both be safe.* The aftershocks would be bringing more bricks and concrete down all the time. There'd be no lights on in the city. How would she see in the dark? I was so glad she had my shoes.

Prof's nephew turned up around ten. His car had five people in it already but they squeezed Prof in. They were going to their holiday house at Wanaka. He wasn't a huggy man, but each of us got a handshake. 'Thank you, dear people. And please – use anything from my house. Help yourselves.'

It was an hour later when Alex Jaffrie drove up in their car. I wished again that it was Dad and I wished he was hugging me and Blake like Alex was hugging Cindy and Caroline.

He ate three sausages and a slice of thawing cheesecake, and downed two cups of tea. 'We'll drive to Dunedin in the morning if the airport here's not open. Grab a flight to Auckland from there,' he told his family. Their son Evan lived in Auckland. Lucky Evan to live in a city where the earth didn't crack under your feet.

'Give the airport a call,' I said. 'The landline works.'

That led to a flurry of other calls.

Marlene Chan rang her parents. When she hung up, she said, 'They'll come and get us tomorrow.' She looked at her husband, a question in her face.

Robert shook his head. 'I'm staying. I'll be able to help.' He was an engineer and he'd worked non-stop for days after September. Their house had been only slightly damaged then but now it was a wreck and they wouldn't be able to live in it. Oh well, chuck another mattress on the floor, Lyla.

Aftershocks kept rattling the house and all of us with them. I was glad it wasn't just Blake and me here by ourselves.

Towards midnight Natalie came back from the medical centre. We gave her food.

'What's it like out there?' Caroline asked.

Natalie shook her head. 'Bad. Lots of injuries. We couldn't get into our building, so the medical staff were stitching people up under car lights. We had a couple of makeshift tents for the worst cases. I was running all over the place with the supplies we managed to salvage.

Kids were crying. People were in shock. It's just awful.' She broke down in tears.

Marlene and Cindy rushed to comfort her but we all knew there was no comfort in our city that night.

Matt, Marlene, Robert, Natalie, the Jaffries – all of them stretched out on the mattresses but only the kids slept. I squashed into a lounge chair with Blake who sighed but didn't shove me out. At one point, Matt said, 'Aftershocks feel different when you're lying down, Lyla. You should try it. And by the way, good job on the rescue even if it did take you forever.'

I struggled not to cry. Matt was being kind! I knew he was trying to distract me.

'Any time,' I told him, and actually managed a smile when he shuddered. 'You okay?'

'I'll live.'

Time crawled on. The reports coming over the radio were awful.

Sixty-six people were dead and the number would get higher.

People were trapped in damaged high-rise buildings in the central city. One of Greer's cleaning jobs was in a high-rise block of flats. Joanne could have been in a city high-rise.

There were multiple fatalities throughout the city.

There was only one survivor from a bus crushed by a falling building.

Rescuers were working under floodlights in the cold,

desperately trying to find people in the ruins. It was summer. Why was the weather so wintry? It seemed to me that nature had turned against us today.

I went to the window to look out. The floodlights must be powerful. Beams of light reached upwards into the darkness from the central city. Everywhere else was totally black.

Urban Search and Rescue teams were on their way from other countries. A team from New South Wales would be here by morning.

Mum wasn't part of a USAR team, but I knew that wouldn't stop her. She'd still be searching through rubble.

Blake's arm around my shoulders comforted me.

'They'll be all right, Lyla.'

I wished they'd come home.

Eight

All night long the house groaned and shuddered. It felt like its sinews were being stretched to breaking. Leo woke in a panic, not knowing where he was, and Natalie wrapped her arms around him. 'It's all right. It's just Rūaumoko, but he's not really angry. We're safe. I promise.'

Matt looked like he was in pain. I stretched out a foot to touch his shoulder. 'Want some drugs?' I should have thought of that earlier – but he could have asked too.

He turned his head to whisper, 'What you got?'

'Codeine. If I can find it.'

'Find it.'

It was where everything else was by now, on the floor. The doors on the bathroom cabinet were swinging gently. I left them open – nothing left in there now.

Matt chugged down a couple of tablets. 'Lyla, also known as Girl Friday.' From Matt, that was a heartfelt thank you.

You go kind of numb after a while, at least I did. My mind sort of shut down – nothing going on, nobody home. It was easier that way.

I might have gone to sleep, because I got the mother of all frights when Blake started pushing and shoving. 'Hear that? It's a car. Come on, Lyla – let me up, will you!'

I didn't need telling twice. We leapt over bodies and raced for the front door. Blake snatched up a torch. We got that door open in record time and hurtled outside.

I couldn't make sense of what I was seeing. Ghostly figures in the dark. A big truck – an *army* truck?

'Blake! Lyla!' Then Mum was running. We all crashed together in a massive, blubbery hug.

I kept saying, 'You're still alive! You're okay? Dad? Have you heard from Dad?'

She shook her head. 'He'll be doing triage at the hospital. Don't worry, Lyla. He's fine, I'm sure he is.'

But she didn't know for sure.

We shut the door as much as we could and I only noticed the two extra people when we were back inside. Mum introduced them. 'Karen and Winston. Doctors from Australia. Dead tired.'

Marlene half sat up. 'Good to see you, Clemmie. Welcome to the Ireland Street Marae.'

'September all over again,' Mum said through a massive yawn.

I offered tea and food but they didn't want anything except sleep. 'People have been bringing us stuff – cakes, pies, muffins. Coffee.'

Somehow, the Aussie doctors found space to lie down. Matt gave up his mattress. 'I'm good at sleeping – can do it anywhere.'

Blake and I followed Mum to her room and watched her fall onto her bed – I don't think she even noticed the mattress wasn't there, just like the duvet and pillows weren't. She was wearing overalls and a fluoro jacket, both too big for her. She still had my shoes on. The sight of them reminded me of the grandparents, all four of them waiting to hear Mum and Dad were okay.

I groaned, and whispered to Blake, 'Gotta ring the grands.' No need to whisper, though – a cannon blasting off wouldn't have woken Mum.

In the end, I just rang the Wellington grands and whispered into the phone, 'Mum's home, but Dad's not. Mum says he's probably working at the hospital, but can you ring Grandy and Nana Lilith? I'm too tired.' But it wasn't that. I didn't want to be the one to tell Dad's parents that we didn't know if he was still alive.

Blake had taken the shoes off Mum when I got back. He'd pulled the emergency sleeping bags from the wardrobe, and we tucked one around our mother's grubby-but-alive body. Dad's sleeping bag lay on the bed ready for him if he turned up before morning.

It was the floor for us. I raided the wardrobe for pillow substitutes. Blake was happy with a rolled-up fleece of Dad's. I used Mum's fluffy dressing-gown.

Mum hadn't been killed. Dad was probably alive – he would be, he definitely would be still alive.

Morning happened before I was ready for it. It turned out you couldn't keep an emergency response worker in bed when there were people to help. Mum was up and rattling around far too early.

I opened my eyes. 'Dad? Has he texted?'

Mum shook her head. 'No, but texts aren't getting through yet. Don't worry, darling. They've called on all medical staff to go to the hospital if they possibly can. You know Dad – that's where he'll be.'

I burst into tears. 'Sorry, sorry. I'm just so scared! I saw all that stuff in town and there were dead people and blood and there's people stuck in that building and…'

My mother hugged me until I stopped crying. 'Sorry.'

'Shh,' she said. 'Nothing to be sorry about. I'm sorry you had to see such terrible sights. Were Katie and Shona with you? Are they okay?'

I shivered. 'They were, but I can't get hold of either of them now. Shona was worried about Greer too because Tuesday's her cleaning day and she didn't know where she'd be. I don't know about Joanne, either.'

Mum stroked my head. 'It could just be that Shona and Katie's families have had to relocate. The damage and liquefaction are terrible over in Dallington, and it's pretty bad in streets near the Avon.'

That made me feel marginally more hopeful, but I couldn't bear to tell her Joanne had been in town, possibly in a multistorey building.

Mum tipped my chin up so that she could drill me with her Mother-Gaze. 'Honey, I should go back to work. But tell me the truth – will you be okay or will you worry yourself sick about Dad?'

I tried to smile. Epic fail. 'I'll be okay. Leo and Henry are good distractions. Matt's here too, don't forget.'

She looked uncertain but turned to Blake. 'What about you, Blake? What's happening with the army?'

She meant the Student Volunteer Army that got set up via Facebook to help after the September quake. Blake had joined thousands of other students armed with shovels and wheelbarrows to dig liquefaction out of houses and streets. By the sound of it, all the liquefaction they'd dug out was back.

Blake actually sat up. 'Dunno yet. But I'll go if things are up and running.'

'Mum, those doctors you brought with you last night – are they on holiday?'

She gave up trying to make her hair look halfway decent. 'No, they were here for a conference. Karen's from Adelaide. Winston's a Tasmanian.'

I thought back to yesterday. The woman who'd tended to Ian in Latimer Square had an Aussie accent. 'Are they emergency doctors?' It seemed too good to be true.

Mum gave a bit of a grin. 'Not so much. They're urology surgeons. There's a bunch of them here for a conference.'

Blake patted my head. 'Urology, my innocent little sister, is human plumbing. Wees and associated organs.'

Huh? 'But...how would they know about triaging injured people?' You wouldn't meet any injuries being a wees doctor. I didn't think so, anyway.

Mum changed the subject. 'Lyla, do you want to go to Wellington? The grandparents would love to have you.'

I knew that was true. 'No. I want to stay here. I want to help.'

'Not with the Student Army,' Blake said. 'I'm not babysitting you, so don't even think about it.'

That wasn't worth wasting words on, but in any case Mum agreed. 'No to the army, Lyla.' She held up a shushing-type hand. 'Not because you'd need looking after, but you are only thirteen and they'll be doing extremely heavy and exhausting work. There's plenty to do round here if you want to help.'

'I can do it! And I'm nearly fourteen. My birthday's next month, just in case you've forgotten.'

'The students are older than you. Yes, I know – some high-school kids were among them, but you're not going to be one of them.'

I opened my mouth, then shut it. Mum was tired, and there were new lines on her face. *Don't add to the stress, Lyla.* I wanted to say it'd keep me from worrying myself sick about Dad, but I managed not to.

'All right, I'll stay here. I don't want to, but I'll do it.'

Her whole body relaxed and tears came to her eyes. I got hugged. I felt like a noble martyr until Blake said, 'You're not strong enough to man a shovel anyway.'

I still didn't bother wasting words on him.

We went out to join our refugees in the lounge. Everyone was up off the floor. The mattresses were stacked in a corner with Henry, Leo and the Chan kids using them as a trampoline. We followed the scent of food floating in from the barbecue.

The Aussie doctors were out there looking tired, hands wrapped around steaming mugs. Matt was sitting on a cushion from the sofa. A large crack ran from the roofline of the wall he was leaning against and disappeared behind his back. His ankle was neatly bandaged. Dad's industrial-sized first-aid kit was beside him. 'Sprained, not broken,' he said when he saw me looking.

Silent questions zapped between Marlene, Natalie and Mum; a tipping of the head plus raised eyebrows meant *any news of Geoff?*

Mum's quick headshake said far more to me than just *no.*

I had to do something, find a distraction. I went to see if Marlene needed help at the barbecue. She grinned at me. 'Fancy pita bread for breakfast, Lyla? Fillings over there.' She waved her spatula at a heaped plate of bacon, tomatoes, sliced pizza and potato fries. I filled three pitas for Matt, one each for the little boys and forced one down my own throat, but only because I knew Mum's eagle eyes were watching me.

When she saw I was eating, she turned to Marlene. 'Where's Robert?'

'Getting what he can out of our house. He's borrowed Geoff's gumboots.' She whacked the spatula down against the hot plate. 'I wish I could stay and help, but with the kids it's just not practical.'

The radio was on. There was an announcement about the Student Army. Basically it said *don't come until tomorrow.* Blake shrugged. 'Fine. I'll check on a couple of mates. Might stay at theirs tonight. They've probably got water.'

Water. Showers. Envy.

Useless to think about it. I longed to ask the doctors about yesterday, about who they'd helped – but there would have been people they couldn't help. I kept my mouth shut.

I'd find some way to help, and it wasn't going to be just hanging around home looking after Leo and Henry. Mum was out there making a real difference. Tomorrow, Blake would be too. I hoped that was what Dad was doing right now.

Nine

Life doesn't get put on hold for an earthquake – well, normal life does, but the new normal gets into gear and launches off at a million kilometres an hour.

Things kicked off with Natalie. She looked at her boys, glanced out the window (the weather had improved on yesterday's effort, cloudy with sunny patches), back at her boys, took a deep breath and said, 'They want us at work if we can possibly get there.'

The boys wailed. It was my turn for the deep breath. 'It's okay, Natalie. I'll look after them. They're awesome dudes. I'm glad they'll be here to keep me company.'

I got a massive hug from her and then from both boys. 'I love you, Lyla,' said Leo.

'I really love you, Lyla,' said Henry.

Great – competitive loving.

But from Matt: 'I don't love you, Lyla.'

Oh yeah, he'd be hanging around too.

We watched all the big people, the ones who could be in charge of their own destinies, depart and the Chan girls grizzled about going with their mum. 'Daddy's staying, so why can't we?' Imelda glared at Marlene, hands on her hips.

Then Henry and Leo turned to me. 'What are we going to do? We can't go to school.'

And there was Matt grinning away all over his smug excuse for a face clearly relishing the prospect of watching me kid-minding all day, plus he'd be sliding in the snarky comments whenever he could which would be every two seconds.

I ignored him. 'We're going to be just like the Student Volunteer Army. We're going to be the Street Volunteer Army, and we're going to clean up around here.'

I swear Matt looked disappointed, but I could have wronged him because after a few seconds of deep thought he said, 'That's not a bad idea. We'll get stray kids to help.'

I liked his use of the word *we*. I liked it so much I found a tramping pole to help him hobble around.

'First, we scout the neighbourhood,' I told my troops.

And off we went, with me trundling the wheelbarrow as best I could over the broken street. The boys carried their beach spades – metal ones, not plastic, thank goodness. To begin with, they stuck close to me and Matt, but by the time we reached the end of Ireland Street they were competing to see who could jump the furthest over the cracks in the footpath. The shaking ground didn't spook them the way it did when they were in the house.

The immediate neighbourhood was just like our street – some places fully munted, some looking liveable and some drowning in liquefaction up to their window-sills. Matt stomped along, swearing just loud enough so the kids could hear. They giggled and jumped – excellent. But he looked at me and pulled a face. I nodded. Yes, it was bad here, and worse in the city. He didn't say dumb stuff about Dad – just one muttered comment. 'Geoff had better bloody well turn up today.'

For some reason that was hugely comforting. Weird.

We passed lots of people out with shovels and wheelbarrows but they all had plenty of manpower until we got a couple of streets away, where we saw an old couple digging a path through the gunk from their front door. They hadn't cleared much. You could tell the work was too heavy for them.

'Hi there,' I called. 'Can we help? I'm Lyla, this is Henry and this is Leo.'

Matt could introduce himself. And sure, he did the *hi I'm Matt* mumble but then off he hobbled. Seemed that the transformation from Matt the Horrible to Matt the Okay had only lasted a day. Oh well, what did I expect?

The old couple said to call them Dave and Myra. 'You absolute darlings,' Myra said. 'You've no idea what it means to see your smiling faces.'

'And we're mighty glad of the help,' Dave said.

We got to work. Liquefaction is heavy, and when it dries out the dust gets in your mouth and nose. This stuff was still wet enough to stick together in clumps, a bit like digging wet sand at the beach. I thought the boys wouldn't keep at it for more than five minutes, or else they'd get spooked again by the shaky ground, but they didn't give up. They dug those spades into the gunk and slapped it into the wheelbarrow.

'What excellent workers you've brought us, Lyla. We're so lucky!' Myra said.

We'd cleared maybe a metre of the path when Matt came limping back, followed by a whole tangle of kids armed with wheelbarrows, buckets, spades and grins.

'Your brain's not damaged then?' I said, but I was grinning too. More was definitely merrier, especially as I recognised Millie and Jessica from the year below me at school.

Millie dug into the sludge beside me. 'Dad says Avonside Drive's a total disaster. He reckons the school will be badly damaged.'

It couldn't be too bad, surely. It had survived the September quake and we'd only had a few days off until it reopened. GG Block would be fine this time too. It had to be, it was our history – the school's and my family's.

Dad would be alive and well too. He would be. He absolutely had to be.

I concentrated on the shovelling, barrowing and dumping of gunk onto the kerb.

Matt perched himself on an intact part of the stone wall, making jokes and encouraging the little kids with dumb remarks. 'Look at those muscles, man! Hey, you can join my de-gunking gang. Not much pay, but excellent gunk to shift.' It seemed to work.

Dave and Myra worked alongside us, but they had to pause several times. 'You don't know how good it is not to be alone. Thank you a thousand times.'

Once the entire front path was visible again we stood round leaning on our shovels and trying to look like properly humble heroes, but Matt got off his chuff and hobbled towards Dave and Myra. 'How's the long-drop situation?'

They glanced at each other. 'We haven't been able to get to it.'

Ick! I didn't ask what they'd been using instead, and I didn't argue when Matt beckoned to three boys he seemed to know. 'Come on, guys. Follow me.'

The rest of us began the Great Garden Clearance. I deployed my troops strategically. Millie and Jessica got helped by the eight-year-old twins Jendi and Paul. Henry and Leo stayed with me. I set the five slightly older kids to work on the rockery.

Dave and Myra walked along their newly cleared path and off down the road. 'Back soon,' Dave said.

We watched them go, just walking away as though nobody was slaving away for their benefit. Paul said, 'They should be helping.'

'They're old and they've had a big shock, so don't be mean, Paul Marsh,' Jendi said.

'We've had a big shock too, so you shut up, Jendi Marsh.'

That's all I needed – twin warfare. Things got worse. 'I'm thirsty,' Leo said.

And so was everybody else. 'This isn't fun,' one of the ten-year-olds said.

I called a halt. 'Take a break, soldiers. Earthquakes aren't fun. You've all been totally awesome. But it's fine if you want to go home.'

Jendi prodded her brother. 'Nah, we'll stay. Home's no fun either.'

One by one, those kids picked up their shovels and we got to work again.

Matt had just led his loo crew from the backyard when we heard a car pull up at the kerb. Somebody we didn't know was driving, but it was Dave and Myra who hopped out of the passenger seats. 'Anyone want a lemonade? We've got cake, muffins and biscuits too.'

And hand sanitiser. All of us knew the drill from last time round when there'd been no water for washing – keeping your hands bug-free was essential if you didn't want to get sick.

I ripped the tab off my can. 'Don't tell me there's a supermarket open already!'

Dave shook his head. 'We found a dairy. The front of the shop had a big gap where the window had come away from the frame, but they were letting people in two at a time, cash only and no change given.'

Same old, same old – no electronic transactions for goodness knows how long. Lucky for us that Dave and Myra still used old-fashioned cash.

That was the best can of lemonade ever. It washed the grit from our mouths, dealt with the thirst and put grins on our dusty faces. I discovered, though, that eating a lunch of sweet stuff makes you long for meat and veg.

We stopped work around the time we'd normally finish school. Dad could be back home by now, but if he wasn't I'd need to keep busy or I'd go nuts. Last night it had been good to have lots of people around, so I sent the kids off home with instructions to tell their parents there'd be a barbecue in our street if they wanted to come.

Myra and Dave held hands, their eyes full of tears. 'We'll be there. It's just so good not to be alone.'

We set off for home. Henry leant against me. 'I'm tired, Lyla. Can I ride in the wheelbarrow?'

'Don't think so, buddy. I'd probably tip you into a sinkhole.' I gave the barrow a heave over a chunk of footpath. 'It's not far. Reckon you can make it?'

He kicked a lump of concrete to send it splodging into the road. 'I *hate* earthquakes!'

Didn't we all.

Matt clomped along with Leo beside him. All of us were tired, filthy and thirsty again.

There was a light on in the lounge when we reached my house. Matt and I stopped dead, staring at it. 'Electricity? We've got power already?' Dad might be home too.

We hurried inside and Matt flicked a switch. The lights came on in the entry hall. 'Yes. Real genuine electricity.'

I ran to my parents' bedroom. It was empty. Worry and disappointment crashed into me.

I felt sick as I trudged back to the others. Matt did the raised-eyebrow thing. I did the headshake.

Leo plonked down on the sofa. 'Can we watch telly, Lyla? Please!'

They weren't allowed to watch television in the day-time normally, but this was the new normal. 'Sure can. Let's see if it still works.'

Matt helped me get the TV upright and set it up with the right cables in the right holes, but we left it on the floor. The aftershocks we were getting would only knock it off its cabinet again.

We turned it on and squished in with the boys to settle down to whatever kids of six and eight like to watch. But this was the new normal, and what we got was earthquake coverage. It was ghastly seeing the devastation in the central city. Henry started crying. Leo's body shook in great tremors. Matt pointed the remote and the screen faded.

'Let's go over to your house,' I said to the boys. 'We'll see if we can find your DVDs.'

I knew Matt would turn the telly back on the second we were out of the house. I'd have done the same.

We took our time sorting through the mess next door and I made sure we created enough noise when we came back to warn him to switch it off again. But it wasn't off. Matt had paused it on a quake image. 'Um?' I looked at him. 'What? Why the grin?'

He picked up the remote. 'Take a look at this.'

The picture rolled for three seconds before he paused it again – on a close-up of my father's face. He was talking to a kid of about four, showing her something out of shot.

'Dad! He's alive! Matt, he's alive!' I wanted to reach into the telly and hug Dad. I wanted to cry and shout and dance. I just danced.

'Thought you'd be pleased,' Matt said. 'There was just that one shot and he's at the hospital. I only had the recorder going because I wanted to check everything was working okay.'

I grinned at him. 'Shall I hug you?'

'Um. No.' Matt gave a shudder of horror. It made me laugh.

'Lyla, can we watch *Toy Story* now?'

For a horrible moment we thought the DVD player was broken, but between us we got it going. The kids went into zombie mode, staring at the screen. Leo hugged a cushion. Henry had his thumb in his mouth. Too bad about the dirt.

Dad was alive. My father was alive and well, he really was.

I got everybody a drink of water. Our supply was dwindling.

Matt and I relocated to the kitchen once the boys were fully absorbed in the telly.

Good news does wonders for the appetite. We sat at the kitchen table scoffing a bag of kumara chips. 'Looks like you've got messages.' He nodded towards the land-line phone.

I picked up the receiver and pressed the appropriate buttons. 'Matthew, it's your mother. Your father's going to check our house and you're to come back to Oamaru with him afterwards. No arguments. You can stay here with us. Jed and Fiona say they'll love to have you.'

'Not happening,' he said. 'Absolutely zero not happening.' He deleted the message.

'Plenty of floor space here,' I said. Huh, the quake must have affected my brain, but when I thought more about having him around it felt okay. Strange, weird and unbelievable.

There was another message, for me this time. It was from Katie. She was crying. 'Lyla, we're leaving Christchurch. Our house is wrecked. We're going to Nelson. We're going to live there for good.'

No! I couldn't be losing my friend.

I put my head down on the table. The three of us had been friends forever. Life wouldn't be the same without Katie. What if Shona, Greer, Joanne...

A savage wave of earthquake hate hit me with seismic force. Why did this have to happen to my city?

Ten

We heard a car pull up outside. The little boys rushed into the kitchen, huddling into me, watching wide-eyed as Matt hobbled to the front door. He yanked it open and there was Mr Nagel, arms out to hug – which Matt let him do for at least half a second. 'Good to see you're fit and well, son,' his dad said with a crooked grin. 'Thanks for putting up with him, Lyla.'

'S'okay.'

Leo, Henry and I stayed at the front door, staring at the two of them. Matt leant on his father and limped across the gluggy road.

'Is Matt going away?' Leo asked. Poor kid, he was trembling all over.

I put an arm around him. 'He wants to stay here with us, but his mother wants him to be with her.'

Henry sniffled. 'I don't want Matt to go away.'

'He should stay,' Leo said. 'He doesn't want to be with his mum. She's a nutcase.'

I winced, but let it pass. Anyway, Leo possibly heard that from Matt himself.

The phone rang and of course I grabbed it – it could have been Katie or Shona or Dad. But I'd barely got the receiver to my ear before I copped another blast from Mrs Nagel. 'Put Matthew on, Lyla.'

No please or thank you. I should tell her it was me who rescued her little darling. 'He's over at your house with his dad.'

'Go and get him. At once, if you please. I need to speak to him urgently.'

Wow! She'd never been as rude as this before; she must be seriously bent out of shape. 'I'll give him your message when he gets back. Sorry, gotta go now.' I put the phone down while she was mid-squawk. It rang again straight away.

The boys swivelled their eyes between it and me. I grinned at them and they fell about giggling as we listened to it ring, laughing all the harder when we heard her voice boom from the answering machine. 'Pick up, Lyla. At once. Do you hear me?'

When the message finished I took the receiver off the hook. Spare me from panicking mothers.

Matt and his dad came back eventually, lugging a box full of semi-frozen food, a water container and a bag of Matt's clothes.

Leo bounced up to Matt. 'Your mum's real mad with Lyla.'

Matt lowered himself onto a chair. 'Jeez! Why can't she leave me alone?'

Henry pressed play on the answer phone. Mr Nagel sighed. 'Give it here, will you, Henry?'

He wiped the message, then dialled his wife. It probably rang for a nano-second before she answered. 'Matthew! Have you packed? Don't forget your...'

Mr Nagel said, 'Cut it out, Liz. Take a deep breath and listen. Matt's fine here. He's doing a great job helping out. No – he wants to stay and I've said he can. And please stop harassing these good people. No more calls.'

He put the phone down, then turned to me. 'I'm very grateful to you, Lyla. Thank you for rescuing my son.'

What could I say to that? *No worries – he was just lying around?* I settled for staring at my feet and muttering something dumb. Mr Nagel reached out and gripped my shoulder, then did the same for Matt – on his unbruised side. 'Take care, son.'

The boys ran to the window to watch him leave. I looked at Matt. 'Your mum a bit overprotective?'

'Whatever gives you that idea?' He shrugged – then winced. 'Must remember not to do that for a bit. Dad's good. Tries to keep her off my back.'

Blake arrived home. I ran to meet him, yelling, 'Dad's okay! He was on the telly. He looked fully tired, but he was still working.' I rattled off the details.

My brother stopped dead, let the news sink in, then grinned at me. 'Awesome. Best news ever.'

'You didn't find a shower then?' He wouldn't have got quite so filthy just riding home on his bike.

He waved a newspaper at me. 'Can you believe it? They published *The Press* this morning!'

'Impressive!' Matt spread it open on the table. I took one look – so many photos, so much destruction and so many deaths. There were sixty-six as of last night, but there would be more by now. This was my city. It was real. This had happened to us. I don't know if I was finding it too hard to believe or if I just didn't want to believe it.

I read through the list of worst-hit suburbs. Dallington, Shona's suburb, was still without power. They'd had bad liquefaction after September, but just being without electricity didn't sound too serious. I wished she'd get in touch. Surely she would've got home safely, and her mother would have been okay too because she worked out at Ilam at the university. Blake had said there was damage there but nothing too dreadful. But I wanted to know for sure and certain that Shona was okay and that Greer had turned up.

'Blake, Greer hasn't messaged you, has she?'

'Greer? No, why should she?' He glanced at me, and saw some expression on my face that made him add, 'I'll tell you if she does.'

Matt stabbed at the page. 'Jeez, imagine being that guy.'

It was a rescue story. Somebody had watched four people carry a badly hurt man on a slab of plywood to a police car. The plywood was too big to go in the car, so the four of them held him on top of its roof while the cop drove slowly to the hospital over those terrifying roads.

In the central city the ground was like jelly and shaking all the time.

There was some good news. Soldiers, a thousand of them, were in the city helping. USAR crews were on their way from all over the world. The New South Wales team was already here.

I looked for news of my school, but there was nothing.

Matt pushed the paper away. 'A category 3 state of emergency. Not good, Lyla.'

I didn't know if it was better to watch TV and listen to the radio, or if it was better not knowing what was happening. Neither seemed good.

Blake said, 'You dudes know why peeps are heading towards ours lugging barbies and food?'

Leo scrambled up to perch by the window. 'We told them to, cos it's fun to have a party.'

The pressure inside me eased. It was good to have people around. There was a collection of four barbecues and all the families from our work crew. Somehow, we'd all get through this. I went out to meet them. It was lucky the evening wasn't cold because there were too many of us to fit in the house.

Mum came home just as the food was almost ready to eat. I ran out to her. 'Dad's okay! We saw him on telly. He's at the hospital.'

She stopped in mid-stride, her hands flying to her mouth. 'Truly, Lyla? You're sure?'

I flung my arms around her. 'Positive! Matt recorded him.'

She gave me a shaky smile. 'I just might have to hug Matt.'

I laughed and threaded my arm through hers. 'Where are the Aussie doctors?'

'On their way home. They were fantastic yesterday, but we've got enough local medical staff now so they figured it was best for them all to get out and not be a burden on the city.' She sank down on the picnic chair Blake shoved at her. 'Thanks, kids. This is such a good thing to do.' She gestured at the crowd standing around on our back lawn. It was like a party, lots of laughing and even some singing. Looking at us, you'd never guess at the horrible stuff we all had to deal with.

I ate my share of pizza, sausages, chips and a cob of corn and tried not to think of the bad stuff. I should have contacted Joanne – told her to bring her family. *Come on, brain – kick into gear, why can't you?*

Dad came home just as it was getting dark. He was tired, dead tired, but he was alive and hugged the three of us as if he'd never let us go. Okay by me.

Eleven

In the morning I sat up in a hurry. Had I dreamed Dad was back and okay? Phew. That was no dream. He was here, lying on his back with his mouth open. My dad, alive and gently snoring.

I got up when Mum, Natalie and Robert started walking over me. That night nine of us had slept in the lounge – my family, Natalie and her boys, Robert Chan and Matt. None of us had had a shower since yesterday morning and there wasn't enough water to use for a bucket bath, but who cared? Dad was alive!

However, soon my mind turned to Shona. Why wasn't she telling us she was okay? Had she lost her phone – dropped it in a sinkhole, or was the battery flat? Dallington mightn't have power back on yet. I needed my friends. I sent yet another text: *Shona, where are you? Please. Get in touch.*

The day swung into busyness. The radio was going. The national anthem was playing, the final verse.

Tōna pai me toitū
Tika rawa, pono pū;
Tōna noho, tāna tū;
Iwi nō Ihowā.
Kaua mōna whakamā;
Kia hau te ingoa;
Kia tū hei tauira;
Aotearoa

I started singing along – it was either that or cry. The boys – and Matt, to my gobsmacked astonishment – joined in. Then the announcer said, 'Kia kaha, Christchurch,' and that finished me off. I swiped at my tears and hugged the boys. 'Kia kaha, Leo. Kia kaha, Henry.' *Be strong.* We'd get through this, somehow.

It was Thursday – only two days since the world went crazy. We listened to the news as we got on with the day. Thousands of people were getting out of the city. The airport had reopened and there was chaos in the terminal. Shona could be there with her mum. Greer would probably stay to work with the Student Army.

I flicked a light off – and a lightbulb went on in my brain. If this quake was like September then there'd still be lots of places without power. 'Hey, guys, we're going to open our very own electricity phone-charging station. Who's going to help me make some signs?'

We all got into it. *Charge your phone! Boil a kettle! There's power at 12 Ireland Street.* Matt drew big hollow letters with a black marker, for Leo and Henry to colour in. 'Sometimes you even have a reasonable idea.'

High praise.

We searched the house for a table, extension cord and multi-plug. Matt could man our charging station while the rest of us shovelled the street clean.

The kids helped tack our four signs up at nearby intersections where we couldn't see any evidence of the power being on. I was wondering if we should go and look for our liquefaction workforce when Jendi and Paul's mother turned up. 'Lyla, how about I take the boys with me today? A few of us are having an activity day for the local kids. I've asked Natalie and she says it's fine with her if you don't mind.'

'Thanks.' I definitely didn't mind. 'It'll be good for them to have interesting stuff to do.'

My workforce was down to three: me, Millie and Jessica. Except then the girls swung by to say they were going to help with the activity day. Fine. But I wasn't going to do solo liquefaction.

I set up the table of power with Matt. We had the radio going. It was tough listening to the rising numbers of the dead. Better to focus on the help pouring in from all over the world.

We waited for people to come and use our electricity. I wondered how long it would be before Matt started in with the smart comments about how I should have known everybody round here had power.

Then a boy about his age swished through the liquefaction on his bike. 'Three phones to charge. Okay?'

'Sure, Xave. Help yourself. How's things at yours?'

'Can't live there. Completely wrecked. We've been in the welfare centre at Cowles Stadium. It's rank, man!

Farting. Snoring.' Xave pointed at the radio. 'What's the latest?'

Matt cleared his throat and did a major fail at being a radio announcer. 'Goooood morning, Christchurch – and what a beautiful sunny morning it isn't. Folks, you'll be delighted to know we've had aftershocks overnight. How many, I hear you ask? Not one, not two – but would you believe it – twenty-three of the suckers between nine-thirty last night and six o'clock this morning. And that's only counting the ones measuring from two point nine to four point one.'

Xave shrugged. 'Felt every single one of 'em.'

Then he rode off with his three charged phones.

'Mate of yours?' I asked.

'Does three of the same subjects as me at school. Bit of a rebel. Makes life interesting.'

Five minutes tootled on past, then a very shaken-looking guy walked up carrying his kettle. I took it to plug it in. It felt too light. 'There's hardly any water in here.'

'It's all I've got. I didn't prepare for this.' He rubbed his hands over his face.

'We've still got some. I'll make you a drink. What do you want?'

He wanted coffee. I made drinks for me and Matt too. Between the three of us, we finished up the last of a fruitcake. The guy perked up amazingly and nodded at the radio. 'What's the latest?'

Before Matt could report something scary like how there were now seventy-one bodies and they'd had to set up a morgue at Burnham Military Camp, I said, 'Lots of sympathy from all round the world. The Pope, the Dalai Lama, President Obama, the Queen – messages from all of them.'

The man nodded. 'That's nice. You'd expect it, but it's still nice.' He picked up his kettle and wandered away.

Matt leant back in his chair and tapped a finger on the table. 'Now listen up, young Lyla – you gotta understand I can read people. Better than you, probably. No way was I going to load bad news on Mr Unprepared.'

I used my own finger to bash a drumbeat on the table – better than jabbing him with it, I guess. 'You can read people? Yeah, right. For starters, you wouldn't be doing the *young Lyla* thing, *old Matt*.'

Whatever he'd been going to slay me with next didn't happen thanks to a car pulling up. The driver leapt out. Cool hair – it shone bright purple. She sprinted up the path, waving a bottle in one hand and a kettle in the other, while the other woman in the car unbuckled a crying baby from its car seat. 'Please! Can we get this warm? She won't drink it cold.'

The kettle boiled, the hot water warmed the bottle, and the baby wailed. I brought out chairs for the parents, but we didn't try to talk. That kid was *loud*.

Finally! The milk was warm enough. The baby shut up and drank. The parents breathed out and smiled.

'What's the latest?' Purple Hair asked.

'You want to get out of Christchurch?' Matt asked. 'Air New Zealand's putting on extra planes. Cheap flights.' Fair question because they had Australian accents, so why not go back to the land of stable ground?

Purple Hair's partner shook her head. 'We're staying. This is our city now.'

Uh oh – a roaring sound like a train coming. We all knew that noise only too well by now. I snatched the kettle of steaming water off the table and dumped it on the ground. All of us scrambled under the table. The earth rattled and shook. The baby kept drinking.

When the bottle was empty Purple Hair said we'd saved their lives and they hurried away. We watched their car zigzag away round the liquefaction. The radio reported the strength of the aftershock. It was a four point one.

Matt's mate Xave came flying back a few minutes later, swerving to miss the gunge. He dropped his bike and sprinted up the path. 'Hey, Matt! The Crusaders aren't gonna play on Saturday! They should play. We were gunna smash the Hurricanes.'

Really? Mourning a game of rugby when so many people were dead? 'You reckon they should just jump on a plane as if nothing's happened?' I yelled at him. 'What about their families? They just might be needed at home right now.' *Idiot.*

I waited for Matt to do a *young Lyla* effort, and when he did he was going to get a thumping.

But I nearly fell off my chair without the help of an aftershock when he said, 'Lyla's right, Xave. I'd call if off too if I was captain.'

Xave went away muttering. And I asked, 'Are you captain of the first fifteen?'

He grinned. 'I'm Year Eleven, Lyla. But in another two years – watch this space.'

'You want to be an All Black?' Typical rugby-head boy – of course he wanted to be an All Black.

He closed his eyes and didn't reply. Yep, dreaming about leading his team of players into the stadiums of the world.

People turned up throughout the morning. Three lots charged their phones, two came to boil water and a woman arrived clutching a skirt that she wanted to iron. It seemed a pretty random thing to be worrying about right now, but I found the iron and the board and let her smooth the wrinkles away.

As soon as she was out of earshot, Matt said, 'Seriously? Why the stress about wrinkles?'

I put on a teacher-y voice. 'It's a metaphor, Matthew. She can't iron her life straight. The skirt is a replacement object.'

He leant an elbow on the table. 'Let's make a deal. I don't *young Lyla* you. And you never again call me *Matthew*.'

'Suits me.' But why would the use of his full name get up his nose? Oh yeah, his mother always called him by the full two syllables. That would do it.

Another radio update stunned us both into silence. There'd been a language school in the CTV building – the one that had collapsed and was still burning. Asian students had been studying there and many of them were feared dead.

Matt whispered, 'Eighty to a hundred fatalities. Those poor people.'

I couldn't get even one word past the choking in my throat.

We kept listening. It was a terrible bulletin. There were more people feared dead in other buildings. The USAR teams were concentrating on ten buildings in the central city, though aftershocks kept rolling through and making the searching dangerous. Dogs were being used to find people under the rubble.

Was Shona buried under rubble? Is that why we couldn't get hold of her?

I couldn't bear it. I walked away, leaving Matt to look after the table. I needed to be busy and there was liquefaction to be shovelled up. Matt called out to me, but I ignored him. The liquefaction had dried to silt and dust that flew everywhere. I breathed it in as I shovelled, then breathed in more as clouds of dust volcanoed up when I tipped each load on the side of the street.

I filled the barrow eight times – and yes, I was counting. Anything to stop having to think about the city. Just as I was starting on the ninth load, what did I see Matt do? He got up and limped off, that's what.

'Where d'you think you're going?' I yelled.

'Temper!' he said. 'I'll tell you where I'm going – when you ask nicely.'

I jabbed the shovel back into the silt. He could disappear down a sinkhole for all I cared. And I was *not* crying. What Matt chose to do was his own business.

Then I heard *thump, step, thump* and there he was, standing right in my face. 'There's a water collection point at Phillipstown School. Want to come?'

I kept my leaking eyes on the ground. 'Okay. But what about...'

'I'm off to ask Dave and Myra to man the table. They probably need water too.' He limped away without waiting for a reply.

I wheeled the barrow to the footpath, my mind wheeling too. What was with Matt Nagel, tormentor of any girl who crossed his path? He could have yelled right back at me, but instead he was actually kind. And thoughtful. And problem-solving. Plus, he'd given me time to get myself together.

It was lunchtime. I wasn't really hungry, but Matt would be. I just wanted the comfort of warm food. There was so much sadness. So many unbearable pictures in my head.

I made us cheese toasties and ate mine before he reappeared with Dave and Myra, who brought with them a bag of chocolate biscuits. I ate three; Matt scoffed through five, and then the toastie. They'd turned the radio on before we were out of earshot.

Matt managed the walk by leaning most of his weight on his bike. I trundled the wheelbarrow. I tried to think of something to say. *Thanks for being kind? Sorry I yelled?* In the end I said, 'Were Dave and Myra okay about manning the table?'

'Thrilled to be doing something to help.' End of conversation.

The school wasn't far, but it took us ages to get there. Everywhere we looked there was damage and destruction. Fences lay higgledy-piggledy on the ground. Huge cracks zigzagged through walls. Whole sides of houses leant out at crazy angles. Silt was piled up at the roadsides where people had cleared liquefaction from around their houses. A cat cowered under a drunkenly leaning bush and hissed at us. The eerie thing was the few random houses that looked to be almost untouched even though both their neighbours could be totally wrecked.

There was a queue for water. I scanned the people, looking for anyone I knew. 'Joanne!' I threw my arms around her. 'Are you okay?' we both asked at the same time. Then we laughed and I said, 'Have you heard anything about our school?'

'Just that it's badly damaged. I hope it's not real bad. I so want to get back to normal.' She swallowed hard. 'It won't be normal, though. Amanda's family are moving to Australia. Willa's in Dunedin, and so is Margie. They might come back, but I don't think they will.'

'It just sucks. Katie's moved to Nelson. Has Amanda said anything about Shona? Has she seen her, do you know?' They lived in the same street, so Amanda would know if anybody did.

But Joanne shook her head. 'No. But she said so many houses are wrecked in her street. Jeez. I hope…'

Me too.

The queue moved slowly. Matt had found a couple of guys from his school. And all of us talked to strangers, swapping our stories.

We shuffled closer to the water tanker, and Joanne sighed. 'I know it's such a small thing when there's so much awful stuff happening – but I'd kill for a shower. I've got liquefaction-dust hair. And I keep thinking I'll run to the dairy. I need chocolate.'

The dairy was now a pile of rubble.

Finally it was our turn. We filled our containers and made the trek back home.

Myra and Dave had quite a crowd at the table when we got back. A guy with his arm in a sling and a huge bruise on his face was charging his phone. The other four didn't have anything plugged in. Apparently they were hanging around for the company. It was another half-hour before they all toddled away.

Myra rubbed her hands together. 'We have so enjoyed ourselves! And look – we've got a news summary for you.'

They'd written a list. I couldn't bear to tell them I didn't want to hear any more news, not today, not ever.

Dave read the list out. The first item was good news. An Australian Army field hospital would arrive tomorrow.

The next was a mixture of good and bad. Lyttelton was completely wrecked. The good part was that the HMNZS *Canterbury* had been docked in the harbour when the world went wild and the navy were feeding the people.

Another feel-good item came next. Peter Jackson and the crew making *The Hobbit* were offering to give practical help where they could. The actors and everyone else involved with the movie were shocked and saddened. They sent their thoughts and prayers.

A good but sad item: Auckland was expecting evacuees today off thirty-six flights. I hated that so many people had to leave my city, but at the same time I hoped Shona, Greer and their mum were among them.

‘Thanks,’ I said to Dave and Myra. ‘That was really kind of you.’

Matt didn’t argue when I left him in charge of the table while I helped them take water back to their house. Just as I was leaving them, Dave slapped his head. ‘Where are my brains? We found our old plug-in phone. What’s your number?’

We swapped numbers. Being able to call them whenever – that felt good.

I walked home slowly, slower as I approached my house. I didn’t want bad news. I couldn’t cope with bad news. I wouldn’t ask Matt what he’d heard while I was away. So what did I do the moment I sat down with him at the table? I asked the dumb question, is what I did. ‘Okay, what’s the not-so-good news?’

‘You sure?’ he asked.

‘No. But it’s worse not knowing.’

So he told me, quick, brief and sharp. Body bags were being carried from the CTV site. It wasn’t known yet how many people had been crushed under stone when the cathedral shattered. Three men had died in another church when it collapsed on them.

I turned the radio off and Matt didn’t protest. You could only take so much horrible news. I dreaded what tomorrow morning would bring. It would be two and a half days since the big quake. Surely nobody could still be alive in any of those broken buildings.

That night once the kids were soundly asleep Matt turned on the television just in time for us to see the Education Minister read out a list of badly damaged schools – and Avonside Girls' High and Shirley Boys' High were among them. My school and Matt's. Crap. Absolute and utter crappy crap.

Life wasn't looking like getting back to anything near normal anytime soon.

Twelve

Friday snuck in while I was asleep. Not sure if it was an aftershock that woke me, the sound of heavy rain or the smell of eggs and toast.

Blake was scoffing down three eggs and a pile of toast. Not the best sight to wake up to, plus he was decked out in his fluoro gear ready to ride off into the sunrise and wield his trusty shovel. I pulled my sleeping bag up over my head. I wanted to be him; well, not actually him, but he'd have company and he'd be helping whereas I only had Matt and there wasn't much either of us could do to help fix the mess our city was in.

A small hand tugged the sleeping bag off my face. Henry. 'Lyla, what'll we do today?'

Oh yeah. I forgot. Child-minding duties.

But Natalie rescued me. 'I'm not working today, boys. Don't tell me you've forgotten what's happening this afternoon?'

Both of them leapt in the air clapping their hands. 'Dad's coming home!' Then Leo's face crumpled. 'But our house is all broken and sad.'

Natalie bent down to gather them both in her arms. 'That's why we're going to start cleaning it up. You ready, my soldiers?'

The three of them hurried next door through the rain. Mum said, 'I sure hope Don's plane isn't held up. Those kids will be in bits if he doesn't make it home today.'

'You still haven't told her about the car?' Dad asked.

Mum shook her head. 'She's got enough to worry about. I'll tell her when she asks, not before.'

I shot a look in Matt's direction and neither of us asked for details. Why bother? We knew that car would be flattened under building rubble.

'What about our car?' I asked.

Mum shrugged. 'Same story. We're lucky we weren't in it.'

They gave me longer goodbye hugs than usual. 'You going okay, chickie?' Mum asked, giving me her searching Mother-Gaze. 'I know it's tough on you not being able to get in among it.'

I was in the middle of a brave smile when Dad said, 'Good work yesterday, you two. But don't go off being heroic, especially not in this weather.' He turned to Matt. 'Same goes for you.'

Matt stood tall on his undamaged leg. 'Don't worry, Geoff. I'll keep her in lockdown the whole day.'

I waited till an army jeep had taken the parents off to work before I responded to Mr Matthew Nagel. 'You're going to catch me when I run away to be heroic, are you? Well, good luck with that.'

He hit me with a squelcher of a look. 'They're tired and stressed. They'll both be dealing with dark stuff all day. D'you really want them worrying you'll do something stupid?'

I flopped into a chair. It's easier to bury your head in your hands when you're sitting down. 'Okay! I get it. You're right and I was dumb. Happy now?' Then I waggled a hand at him. 'Sorry. Didn't mean to yell.' My mind shied away from the dark stuff Mum was dealing with. She was working out at Burnham today. The military camp was at Burnham. That was where the emergency morgue had been set up.

I stood up. 'I guess we could rig up something to collect rainwater. Seems a shame to let it all go down the drain.'

'It won't be doing that,' said Mr Get-everything-exactly-correct. I knew the damn drains were broken to hell; I didn't need him to come over all picky.

Silence – eventually broken by Matt saying, 'Water-collecting's not a stupid idea at all, though. Buckets? Bowls? Plastic sheeting?'

Maybe that was an apology. But with Matt, who knew? I decided to believe it was. 'Yes to all of the above. Get the rain gear organised and I'll get the rest.'

'Aye aye, captain. At the double.'

If only.

The bowls were no problem to find, but the buckets and plastic sheets were all in the laundry and I'd stayed well away since Death by Dryer had missed me by minutes.

It's okay.

There's nothing left up high to fall in the next aftershock.

You can do this.

One, two, three.

Four, five, six.

Seven.

Eight.

Nine, ten. Go now!

I made a grab for the two buckets but the plastic could stay in the cupboard. The landline rang as I was backing out. 'Matt, can you get that?' It would be his mother – he could deal with her.

'For you,' he yelled. 'It's your mate.'

Katie? I snatched the phone. 'Katie? Has…'

'It's me. Shona.'

My legs gave way. 'Oh my god! Shona! Are you okay? We've been worried sick.'

She gave a gulp. 'I'm all right. We're in Dunedin. They flew Greer down here. She's hurt…'

I gripped the phone till my fingers ached, as if somehow that would help my friend. 'What happened? How bad is it?'

Matt sat across the table, staring at his locked hands. I was glad he was there. I was so glad I wasn't by myself. It took Shona a moment to get calm enough to speak. 'She'll be okay. At least, they say she will be, but they say she needs to stay calm. She got a head injury.'

We waited again for her to get control of her voice. I pressed the speaker button so Matt could hear. 'Shona?'

'Sorry. We're just so worried. It's her thesis. It's on her laptop. She keeps asking for it and fretting. She should be getting better by now but she's not because she keeps tossing and turning and worrying and not sleeping like she needs to.'

I didn't understand. 'But the backups. She's got two of them, remember? Blake made her back it all up.'

A hiccupping sob came over the line. 'They're gone. She had one of the USBs on a lanyard round her neck, but it got crushed. The hard drive's at home somewhere under all the liquefaction. She's lost all her most recent work!'

'Her laptop's okay, though? I'll go round to yours now,' I said. 'I'll text you when I've got it.'

'But it's not there, it's at her work. She had it with her and the building's a mess. Nobody's allowed in. It's red-stickered. There's a cordon and the army and everything. Could your mum help?' There was so much desperate hope in her voice that I winced. But what if the laptop had been crushed too?

'I'll ask her. What's the address?' Greer's cleaning jobs took her all over the city. She could have been anywhere.

'It's that tower block. The one by the park.'

Which park? Which tower block? 'Have you got an address?'

'Oh. Yes. Sorry. It's the corner of Park Terrace and... oh god, I can't remember. Fifth floor. She said it's the fifth floor.'

'I'll find it. Don't worry. I'll text you when I get it.' I crossed my fingers. Mum would make it happen.

'No phone. I've lost it. I'll ring you again tomorrow if that's okay?'

'Sure. But where are you staying? Have you got rellos in Dunedin?' I wished they'd kept Greer in Christchurch Hospital. Shona and her mum could have stayed here.

'We're with an old couple. Stan and Elsa. They just turned up at the hospital to see if anyone needed a place to stay. They've been driving us here every day and giving us food. People are so kind, but I just want Greer to…' Shona choked up again.

'Don't worry. We'll get it sorted. Tell her enough of the stressing. Love you.'

'Love you too… Dorset Street! It's on the corner. Your mum will know it.'

I hung up, my thoughts whirling because that was better than facing the truth head on.

Matt didn't waste time hiding from the truth. 'Clemmie won't be able to get in there. Army. Cordon.'

'She could ask the authorities. Get permission.' I didn't sound convinced, even to myself.

Matt's face was scornful. 'Yeah? I can just see the military dropping everything to come to the rescue of one laptop.'

'I know, Matt. I know that.' And I did know it. I just didn't want to face it.

Dad's words rang in my head. *Don't go off being heroic.* But Shona had sounded so desperate and I hated the thought of Greer so stressed. I wanted to help. But I knew I shouldn't be stupid enough to break into a cordoned-off, quake-damaged, red-stickered high-rise. I might die in the attempt. Mum and Dad would kill me if I did survive.

But I had to at least try.

Thirteen

I did the deep breathing and stood up, ready to head in the direction of rain gear. Matt gave a grin that went crooked in the middle. 'Looks like I'll be chasing you all the way to the corner of Park and Dorset.'

I collapsed back onto my chair in a rush of relief. 'I could walk slowly.'

'Let's go.'

The rain was sluicing down when we left. 'We didn't put the buckets out,' I said.

'Not going back,' said my trusty companion. Fair enough. I wasn't either.

'How's the ankle?'

'Getting better.'

'You'd say that even if it was falling off the end of your leg.' But I'd be staunch too if Mum flew into a fit at every scratch like Mrs Nagel did. 'It's going to take ages to get to that place.'

'We've got all day.'

Oh well, if he wasn't worried about walking so far I wasn't going to try to stop him.

On any day before the twenty-second of February we'd have cut across the city. We'd have biked on our wide, straight roads with their smooth surfaces. Okay, maybe the smooth surfaces would have to be further back, before the September quake. Today we made our way through sludge and broken streets. No, make that shattered streets full of splits, holes and orange road cones.

I'd have been willing to bet Matt's ankle and probably his shoulder would be hurting. His face was strained and he looked a bit pale. It just about killed me not to say anything, but I kept my mouth shut.

Half a block later we were detouring round a deep hole in the footpath when a car came up beside us. The driver leant on the horn and I died. I swear, my heart stopped, and I wanted to kill the idiot with his hand on the button.

Maybe Matt did too. He bashed the stick against the roof, but then the words he was yelling penetrated my skull. 'Hey, Clancy! Give us a lift, you crazy idiot.'

And miraculous miracle – the car stopped and we fell in, wetness, mud and all.

Matt punched the guy behind the wheel on the arm. 'You're still alive then? Family okay?'

They swapped news for a couple of blocks, then Matt said, 'Your dad know you've got the car?'

Clancy gave him an evil grin, so I figured not. Then I worked out that if Clancy was in Matt's class he was probably only fifteen. I started laughing. It took guts to drive through a city covered in cops when you weren't even old enough to get a licence. I hoped Matt wasn't going to tell him we were on a law-breaking mission too. That guy would be in like a rat up a drain-pipe, and he looked a touch too feral to me.

But yay for feral. Clancy had saved us hours of struggling along horrible streets we no longer recog-nised. I hoped he knew where we were. All the usual landmarks were in bits. Even the cathedral spire wasn't there to guide us. I wouldn't cry, not here in a car full of boys. (Two boys equals a carful, by the way.)

Soldiers and police guarded the roads into the central city. They were there to stop people like us doing exactly what we were hoping to do. We couldn't drive down Bealey Avenue. Clancy wasn't bothered – he swung that car round corners, swerved away from holes, revved it over lumps and cracks.

After an age he pulled up with a jerk which was probably meant to be a flourish. 'There you go, Matt, my old bud. Bealey Ave straight ahead. Hagley Park to your right.'

We made our way down a street which a few days ago had had a name. But when we got within sight of the intersection with Bealey Avenue we stopped. The police had a checkpoint set up.

My heart sank into the sludge at our feet. 'We'll have to wait till dark.' I longed for a café, McDonald's or anywhere, so long as it was warm and dry.

Matt turned around and started walking back the

way we'd come. Well, to hell with him. He could go home, but I was here now and if I had to wait in the rain till night fell then I bloody well would.

He turned to yell at me. 'Are you coming?'

'Okay. Keep your knickers on.' I'd go left at the next intersection and he could limp off back home.

We got to the intersection and he turned left with me, so of course I got all teary-eyed from the relief of having company while I broke every earthquake rule in the book. I thought about saying something. Nah. No nagging and no thanking.

I fully thought there'd be police or army swarming all over the section of Bealey Avenue we needed to walk along. But miracles do happen. There wasn't one single uniform of any sort waiting to block us. We knew they were just down the street at the next crossroads, though, so it was still a bit hard on the nerves.

Matt didn't seem to know what nerves were. He grinned at me. 'This, my friend, is going to be a piece of the old proverbial.'

Yeah, if our luck held. It was eerie. No people. The thump of Matt's stick sounded scarily loud. 'This is the place.' He pointed his stick at a very wrecked-looking tower block. We had to go up there?

Yes, we did. It was Dorset Towers. The high concrete fence in front of the building with the name on it looked like it had never heard of earthquakes. I didn't trust it. One gentle push might send the entire thing crashing down. The tower block of flats behind it looked majorly unsafe – shattered windows, bits fallen off walls, a chunk of the top storey dangling ready to crash to the ground.

We edged around the wall out of sight of the road. I was glad to be sheltered from the eyes of passing officials – not that there seemed to be any.

'How do we get in?' Matt asked.

As if I'd know. 'She didn't say.'

We found the fire escape, a good solid one, but it had a brick wall beside it. 'Lots of cracks in that,' Matt said. He grinned at me. 'Ready to risk your life?'

I shrugged. 'Piece of the old proverbial, like you said.' I wasn't going to tell him my heart had been transplanted with a jackhammer.

He made it up the fire escape to the first floor before he gave up. The gist of what he said was, 'Ankle. Shoulder.' There were quite a few adjectives in there as well.

I swallowed hard a couple of times. 'I'll be okay.' I kept climbing, my eyes turned away from the cracks in the brick wall beside me.

'Remember to count the floors,' he yelled. 'And don't worry – I'll keep the rats away.'

I hoped he was joking.

On three of the floors the doors to the flats had been kicked in. There was a big C scrawled on them. C for clear? C for no bodies. Whoever had done the checking must have found Greer. They'd probably thought she was dead.

The door on the fifth-floor flat was open and undamaged. It had the C on it. I stopped on the threshold and gulped. I wasn't looking at a plain old mess – I was looking at chaos. Ceiling panels were down. I could see where pictures had been on the walls, but there was nothing on them now. Furniture, bookcases, books, the television, CDs – everything was thrown together. The fridge lay facedown in a puddle of water. There was so much water. The hot water cylinder must have spilled its guts along with every single cupboard and drawer in the kitchen and lounge. Splinters of glass glinted wickedly through everything.

I had to find a laptop computer somewhere in all this? I should have asked if it was in a backpack. I should have asked which room it was in.

But I was here now and I wasn't going back without it. *Enough of the procrastinating, Lyla Sherwin. Get on with the job.*

One upside of looking for something in quake rubble is that it doesn't matter if you make it worse. I made it worse.

The first clue was the strap of a backpack. I cleared away books, grains of rice, a wedding photo, a shelf and an armchair before I could free it. Glass fragments shone in the fabric.

I gave the bag a shake, then unzipped it. Yes! The computer was inside. It even had Greer's name etched onto the lid. I wanted to cry. I clasped it in my arms. 'Thank you, thank you, thank you!' I didn't know who or what I was thanking, but it didn't matter. I had that computer and now Greer could get better, Shona could come home and the world would start to feel almost normal again.

I stood up, put on the backpack and took one last look around.

There was a bloodstain on a tiny patch of visible carpet.

Time to get out of there. I scurried back down the fire escape trying not to look at the cracked brick wall beside me. An aftershock rattled the building as I reached the third floor. I sped up.

'What took you so long?' Matt asked as I reached him on the first-floor landing.

'Kill many rats?' I asked.

He did the evil grin. 'Be my guest.' He waved the stick towards the bashed-in door of the first-floor flat.

Talk about party day for rats. A bunch of them were devouring a pantry full of food and they weren't taking the slightest bit of notice of us. 'Okay by you if we get out of here?'

When we reached the ground, neither of us was interested in hanging about. It was still raining and it was going to be a long trek back home.

'Stuff it,' Matt said. 'Don't know about you, but I'm going down Bealey Ave.' Where there were checkpoints manned by cops and soldiers.

I wasn't going to argue. I didn't think the cops would lock us up.

There was an ice-cream van at the checkpoint. 'What the hell?' Matt said.

'Oh man! They're giving out hot drinks. And food.' I was hungry and thirsty. Add wet and cold to that.

It doesn't really work to try doing invisible around

a bunch of cops. One of them gave us the sort of searching look Mum was so good at. 'Okay, you two. Here's the deal. We won't ask what you've been up to if you promise to go right back home and stay there.'

I nodded, too relieved to say a word. Not Matt, though. 'Can we seal the deal with a drink? Food would help too.'

The cop roared with laughter and waved us towards the van. Hot tea, two muffins and a cheese scone later, we were on our way. I didn't even mind that Matt had a smug smile all over his face.

It took hours to get home. He had to stop for a breather several times. I only made one comment. 'There's still a few codeine pills at home.'

He grunted and I spent the rest of the way interpreting what the grunt might mean. *I need more than a few. Thanks for not hassling me about if I'm okay. Keep your mouth shut.* I settled for *thanks.*

We got home. Matt wrenched the door open and collapsed on the couch still soaking wet. I got towels, codeine and water. 'Thanks for coming with me.'

He gulped down the pills. 'Wouldn't have missed it for anything.'

Peace and harmony was alive and well in the Sherwin household, until I said, 'Give me your coat. I'll get some dry trackies for you – if you've got some here?'

'Shut up, Sherwin. You're not my mother.'

'You can die of pneumonia for all I care. But if Mum and Dad come home and see you dripping all over the sofa they're going to ask questions. Blake will too. So have you got spare stuff here or haven't you?'

'Blake's room.'

I marched off and dragged back the plastic rubbish bag full of his clothes. He opened one eye. 'Going to watch me do the down-trou, are you?'

Hopeless. I left him to it while I changed my own clothes for ones that weren't soaking wet and didn't have mud all over them. I'd shed my jeans and had my trackies half on when I heard the rumble of an approaching quake. I scuttled under the doorframe and dropped to do the turtle.

Blasted quakes. Enough already.

It wasn't too bad, about a three point eight at a guess. Thank goodness the earth had more or less behaved itself while I was up in that building. I squeezed my eyes shut, trying to erase the picture of the chaos from my memory. Some hope – it had burrowed deep into my mind.

Lord High-and-Mighty was in dry clothes when I returned. He didn't say anything, and I for sure wasn't going to. I picked up his pile of wet and dirty, chucked it into the laundry and shut the door on the lot. Then I ransacked the pantry, which wasn't hard because there was practically nothing in it.

There was silence from the couch all the time it took me to heat a tin of tomato soup and make a couple of cheese toasties.

Matt scarfed his down – no *thank you, Lyla, you're amazing* from him. He licked both his plates. His only comment was, 'You know, Lyla S, it's going to get tricky if your mate rings when your parents are home.'

I'd already thought about that, and it wasn't a scenario I wanted to dwell on. 'You know what else, Matt N? We've just eaten the last of our supplies.'

He leant back and shut his eyes. 'Life could get interesting round here.'

Hopeless. I had to laugh.

Fourteen

The trouble with a plug-in landline is that you can't take the phone off somewhere private. Various adults including my parents would be home when Shona rang back. I shuddered. I could absolutely see the scene: furious, disappointed parents, plane tickets to Wellington coming right up.

Shona! Ring now! Why haven't you bought a new phone?

Then the solution hit me in the face. Duh! Talk about obvious!

I rang the hospital and asked to speak to Greer Carradine's mother or sister.

I got Shona. 'Lyla? Did your mum manage to get it?' There was so much hope in her voice.

'Yes. It's here. Tell her everything's fine.'

She burst into tears. 'Thank you! Oh, thank you so much – you don't know how much this means.'

'Glad to help,' I said. 'Do you want me to send it down?'

'No. It's okay. We can organise for somebody to pick it up.' She spent some more time thanking me. I was relieved she didn't ask for the full story. She'd be horrified if she knew what I'd done. I just hoped she wouldn't pour gratitude all over Mum.

'Quakes haven't killed all your brain cells,' Matt said when I hung up. He didn't bother opening even one eye this time.

I went to the sink and turned the tap on. Maybe the universe had taken pity on us. Maybe water would gush into the sink. Make that a no.

I thumped my hand on the bench. 'I want a shower. I want to get warm and dry and clean.'

'Typical girl,' Matt said, eyes still shut.

I wanted to kick things too, him especially. I stomped off to my bedroom. I needed my friends. If Shona and Katie were here we'd sit down and have a good hate session on the earthquakes. We'd all feel better and the world wouldn't seem so hideously horrible.

I should dump my dirty clothes in the laundry before they started stinking the place out.

Idea! I laughed, collected them up, stuck my raincoat over my head and ran outside to peg the mucky gear on the clothesline. They'd have to end up cleaner than they were now, even if it would take at least a hundred rainstorms to do it properly. I don't know why, but the sight of my filthy jeans and sweatshirt getting washed by the rain cheered me up amazingly.

I'd just shed the coat when the landline went. I'd have to get it. Matt wouldn't be leaping off the sofa to answer it and it had better not be his mother.

'Hello?'

It was Myra. 'Oh Lyla, I was worried you weren't home. Listen, we had a group of students arrive with food. Could you come and help us bring it to your house? There'll be enough for everybody. Clemmie and Geoff too, if they're hungry when they get home.'

Food? Enough for all of us? My stomach rumbled. 'I'll come right now. We've run out of everything. Thank you so much.' My voice got shaky – the worry about how to feed people lifted.

Myra came over all grandmotherly – told me I was a real soldier, they were so pleased to be able to share with us, I had no idea how much it had meant to them the day we turned up to help clear their yard.

It made me feel warm inside – although still hungry. People *were* kind.

As soon as the phone went down, Matt said, 'They've got food?'

'Sounds like it. See you later.' He didn't argue about coming, which probably meant he was pretty wrecked. Oh well, so was the city.

I sent the parents texts: *Food at ours. Save you some?*

It was not pleasant getting back into wet rain gear, but the lure of food cancelled out the clamminess.

Dave and Myra were all kitted out in coats and gumboots when I arrived. Myra gave me a cheese scone, dripping with butter. 'Straight out of the oven.' She peered at me. 'You look as though you could use a good feed.'

I waggled a hand at her, my mouth too full to get words out. That scone was so good. I closed my eyes to savour the warm butteryness. It tasted of normal, of Sunday brunches when both parents happened to be home and Dad got the cooking urge.

Dave handed me a bag with two big foil-wrapped aluminium dishes inside. 'Lasagne and macaroni cheese. Myra's got chocolate cake and the garlic bread, and I believe I've got quiche and some sort of chilli.'

I scrubbed scone crumbs from my face. 'This should be enough to slow Matt down. For a bit, anyway.'

Myra packed up the rest of the scones too. Off we trudged through the rain. Dave said, 'I guess it's the new normal to be delighted when a bunch of feral-looking students knock on your door.'

Myra said, 'Such kindness. People all over the country want to help. All this food's come from Rangiora.'

When we got home, Matt swore he hadn't fallen asleep. Yeah, right. But he was fully awake enough to chow down four of Myra's scones. I managed another one too – it would have been rude not to.

I was so glad we could cook in the kitchen again. The macaroni cheese and the lasagne were sending out gut-rumbling wafts of fragrance from the oven when Natalie and the boys blew in with Don. Leo and Henry tore into the lounge dragging their dad along between them. Natalie followed, laughing. 'They're a bit excited.'

That would be right. Those kids stayed glued to poor old jetlagged Don, both of them yabbering away, tugging him in different directions to show him the broken window in Blake's room, the long-drop, a hole in the floor in their house, the pile of mattresses.

Don swooped his sons into his arms and the three of them squashed into an armchair. 'You'll have to help me get those mattresses back home. It'll be great to all sleep in our own beds again, won't it?'

That would be a no. Leo got all pale and trembly. Henry wound up like a siren, wailing, 'No! No! No!'

Don looked stunned. He was not in the best shape to cope with two hysterical kids. *Welcome to our world, Don Brunton.*

Natalie knelt in front of her family. 'Boys, listen to me. If it's okay with Lyla we'll stay here, but only if you're quiet.'

'Really?' Leo squirmed round to look his dad in the face. 'You promise?'

'We both promise,' Natalie said firmly. She eyeballed Don until he said, 'Yes. We both promise.'

Blake and Robert Chan arrived together – both of them hungry and dirty.

Myra and Dave helped me serve the food to the starving troops. The ten of us only just fitted round the table. There was silence, except for the scrape of cutlery on plastic and enamel, until Leo said, 'Yum!' Which set off a Mexican wave of *yums* around the table.

Then Matt held up his fork. 'Hear that? Quake approaching.'

And what did we do? Every single one of us, except Don, picked up our plates, slid under the table and kept eating while the earth shook.

Leo pulled at his father's trouser leg. 'Dad, you've got to drop, cover, hold.'

The aftershock and the one that followed it didn't put us off our food. Between us, we demolished all the macaroni cheese and lasagne.

'Boys! Don't lick your plates!' Don sounded disgusted but you could tell he was trying not to show it because he added more gently, 'An earthquake doesn't mean you have to become savages.'

Matt grinned at him. 'Sorry, Don, it's what we do to help clean the plates. Water's a scarce commodity around here.'

Don leant back and shut his eyes. You could just about see the big speech bubble above his head: *I give up.*

My phone buzzed. It was a text from Dad. *I'm well fed. Love you, hon. Thanx for keeping things afloat.*

I re-read the words and was getting all misty-eyed when Robert said, 'Hush, everyone. Hear that? Water's getting in somewhere. Leo, Henry – we need your sharp eyes. We're going on a leak hunt.'

Of course, they shrieked with laughter. So much better than crying and panicking.

Leo found the 'leak'. 'Lyla, look! There's water coming out of the tap!'

Really? It wasn't dripping through a hole in the roof? I couldn't believe it till I saw it with my own eyes. 'Oh, wow!' I held both hands under the tiny dribble of water squeezing its way out of the tap. 'Hey, it's real water!'

The kids and I did a mad whirling dance around the kitchen table. Blake hunted through the cupboards for a bowl to put under the dribble.

Mum arrived home in the middle of the mayhem. I hauled the kids over to the mattresses and dumped them. 'You hungry, Mum?'

She came over to hug me. 'No, I'm all good. The army's great at feeding people.' She turned to Don. 'Glad you got back okay, Don.'

He lifted a hand but, by the look of him, didn't have the energy to get even one word out.

There was a hammering on the front door. Robert went to answer it and came back with a guy I didn't recognise. He introduced himself. 'Wayne Carradine. Greer and Shona's dad. I've just got here from Darwin.'

Please! Don't say anything that'll make Mum ask awkward questions. I jumped up. 'Have you come for Greer's laptop? Hang on, I'll grab it for you. Do you want some food? We've got quiche and cake.'

'No, I'm fine, thanks. I want to get on the road.'

Mum got stern. 'You're not going to drive all the way to Dunedin tonight, are you? Not on top of the travelling you've already done to get this far?'

He shook his head. 'No. Just to Timaru. They say Greer's doing much better since she got the news about her laptop. I can't thank you enough for helping her, Lyla.'

'It wasn't a problem. Glad to help. Tell her to get better.' I made sure my back was to Mum as I frowned at him and tried to get across that if he said any more I'd be in trouble up to my ears.

Mr Carradine was clearly puzzled, but he shut up and just reached out to give me the shoulder squeeze.

I grinned at him. 'Please, will you tell Shona to get another phone and message me?'

'I'll buy her one myself. That's a promise.' And off he went.

I shut the front door behind him and returned to the lounge in time to cop the Mother-Gaze. 'What?' I asked.

'Where did you get that laptop, Lyla?'

I shrugged. 'Mum, don't stress. It was in one of the places she cleans, right where she said it would be.'

'I went with her, Clemmie,' Matt said. 'Made sure she didn't do anything stupid.'

Mum flopped down at the table and did some deep breathing. 'I don't believe either of you. So listen up and listen good. If you pull a stunt like this again – and I'm talking to you too, Matt – then that's it. We'll ship you both out of town. Understood?'

Matt saluted. 'Aye aye, Sergeant Sherwin.'

'I hear you, Mum.' I wondered if she'd noticed that neither of us had actually promised to be good and obedient and sensible. I got the look. Yep, she'd noticed.

I hid out in my bedroom away from Mum's worried frown and suspicious glances but also to avoid ending the day with a catalogue of doom and disaster. It could all wait until the morning. Thank goodness for Facebook. Even if I couldn't be with my friends, we could still hang out in cyberspace.

But Facebook didn't have good news either. Seven girls in my class wouldn't be coming back to school. Their families were leaving for places where the ground didn't shake itself to bits – Auckland, Nelson, Dunedin, Hamilton, Adelaide.

Would the bad news never stop? I logged out without talking to anyone.

Fifteen

In the morning Blake checked to make sure Leo and Henry were out of earshot, then whispered, 'A hundred and twenty-three.'

I pushed my half-eaten food away.

None of us moved for several seconds, then Dad's hand landed on my shoulder in a comforting squeeze. 'Drink your tea, hon. All we can do is keep going. What you and Matt are doing here is worth its weight in fairy dust. You're brilliant, the pair of you.'

How to make a girl cry in one easy lesson.

Blake turned the telly on, just in time to get a police update. 'We are aware of people sneaking into the cordoned area. They may think it's quite clever, but frankly it's stupid and ridiculous. Respect those cordons. They're there for a very, very good reason.'

I felt my mother's x-ray eyes drilling into me. I glared at her. 'I'm not stupid, Mum, so quit giving me the evils, will you!'

It was lucky that Henry barrelled in right then and threw his arms around me. 'We're helping Dad today, but we still love you and we still love Matt.'

I patted him. Matt high-fived him. He shot out the door. Crisis over, because the parents – mine – followed him, laughing. Two minutes later, the house was quiet.

Blake finished off my breakfast. Matt looked at me. 'What's the haps today?'

How come it was my job to figure out Matt's Daily Activity Plan? 'You can please yourself, but I'm on a shower hunt.'

'I know where you could go,' said my dear brother and then, before I could say a word, he hit me with, 'and I'll tell you if you tell me what you got up to yesterday.'

Matt was grinning his stupid head off. 'Stuck between a rock and a hard place.'

Not. I wanted a shower, and Mum had guessed enough to make her suspicious anyway. 'Nothing much. Just went into a cordoned-off high-rise to get Greer's laptop.'

Blake's mouth dropped open. 'Sheesh! You're an idiot. And Matt – you're an even bigger one. I feel like I should stay here and keep an eye on the pair of you.'

'You can do what you like,' I said. 'But just tell me where I can get a shower.'

The rat – he didn't even give me a specific address. 'Head over to the west side of town. There's water on over there. You'll find somebody to let you have a shower.'

Huh, I'd already worked that out for myself. 'You two get outta here. I want to get dressed.'

Matt scuttled off – well, as much as you can when you've got a sprained ankle. But Blake stayed on the sofa and on his phone. 'Not going anywhere just yet.'

A five point six might make him look up – but possibly not. I pulled on yesterday's disgusting clothes, to save my clean ones for after my shower.

Matt reappeared and went to the phone. 'Myra? Matt here. Any chance your friend with the car would help us locate a shower? We'd walk but my ankle's not really up to it yet... Brilliant! Thanks.'

I didn't listen to any more because I got busy collecting clean clothes, towel, soap and shampoo.

'Any towels left?'

From which I figured that a) Matt wanted a shower too and b) Dave and Myra or their car man knew where we could get clean.

Half an hour later, Dave, Myra and friend arrived. Car Man was called Neville and he lived in a retirement place across town. It had water.

We were silent as Neville drove us through a city no longer familiar. So many roads were blocked off. Portaloos dotted the verges of suburban streets. Bridges were unusable. Surfaces that had once been smooth now were shattered. Men driving tractors with big bucket things on them scooped up liquefaction. Myra said, 'The Farmy Army, god bless them.' Farmers, coming in from the country to help us. I waved and blew kisses.

I'll remember that shower for the rest of my life. Te waiora, the healing waters.

Water was precious, so I hurried, but I still had time to savour the warmth along with the sight of dirty suds sluicing off my skin and hair.

I returned to the adults, my hair wrapped in the towel and a grin on my face.

'Feel better?' Neville asked.

'Better doesn't begin to describe it. Thank you so much.'

Matt's phone rang as we were walking back to the car. He checked the screen – and turned the phone off.

'Your mum?' Stupid question – of course it was.

He grunted, then said, 'What's the betting she'll be ringing the landline by now?' He was looking black and fed up. I was glad we were having lunch at Dave and Myra's, because I'd noticed Matt always dealt better with his mother on a full stomach.

Dave and Myra's street had acquired portaloos while we were away. There was one outside their neighbours' place and another one down on the corner.

Matt said, 'If there's one outside my house Mum's going to go ballistic.'

Yeah. She'd think it was *so vulgar.* I was a bit sorry to discover the one in our street was outside the wreck of the Chans' house.

The message light was cheerfully signalling when we got inside. Matt flopped down on the sofa.

'You want to listen?' I asked.

'No.' He slumped further into the cushions. 'Yeah. Get it over with. Hit me with it.'

His mother's voice powered into the room. 'Matthew darling. Call me as soon as you get this. Your father and I aren't going to be living together for the foreseeable future. He won't leave his work and I can't cope with living in Christchurch now. I've bought a house in Timaru. You will live with me, of course.'

Sheesh!

Matt didn't say anything for ages. He scrubbed his hands over his face, then rubbed them through his hair. 'Delete it.'

I hit the button. Okay, his mother was a complete nut job, but really? That was another flaming earthquake.

Then I heard myself say, 'You can stay here.'

The next morning I was up and ready for the day, however many aftershocks it decided to throw at us. My mind was busy thinking about Matt being around for the next few weeks or however long. Funny, I didn't regret it, even though he was still sprawled on his mattress. 'Heard from your dad yet?'

'He'll be here in about an hour.' Then he shot me a lightning-quick look. 'Did you mean it?'

'Yeah, I meant it. Still do.'

He heaved a huge sigh, then I got an almost-grin. 'I'll teach you how to kick a rugby ball.'

'Don't push your luck.'

Don, Natalie and the kids disappeared next door and we turned on the radio. I didn't want to hear more bad news, but couldn't stand not knowing, so I listened.

The death toll had risen. A hundred and forty-five people confirmed dead. Just as bad was the news that the rescue phase had ended and become a recovery operation. I couldn't bear to think about it because it meant they believed nobody in those buildings could still be alive by now. USAR teams were now searching for bodies in the collapsed multistorey office blocks in the city. They were to start the search in the cathedral today. How many had died under those heavy stones?

Mum bent one of her laser-eyed looks on me and shook her head at Dad, who promptly switched the radio off and asked me, 'Lyla, what's the name of that man you helped in Cathedral Square?'

It took me a moment to recall. 'Ian. His name was Ian. MacKenzie. Why?' *Don't tell me he died.*

'I'll see if I can find out what happened to him. If you'd like me to?'

I truly didn't want to know if Ian was dead. But there was only one way to find out. 'Yes. I'd like to know.'

The house emptied out till it was just me and Matt left as usual. I washed the dishes in a bowl – we still had no drains, so the waste water was ending up on the garden. Matt dried them without being asked. Matt Nagel, domestic god. Who'd have thought? 'I'll disappear when your dad arrives,' I told him. They didn't need an audience for private family talk.

I contacted Joanne and we ended up with six of us

from school sitting around outside making popcorn on the barbecue. The things you do.

It was good just hanging out, but it made me miss Katie and Shona so much that I ached.

They all went home for lunch. I went inside and discovered Matt's dad had brought a load of groceries with him. We ate smoked chicken salad, potato salad and fresh bread.

I opened the pantry to find tins of beans, spaghetti, soup, tomatoes, peaches and more all lined up on the floor. There were paper towels, wipes, toilet paper and tissues as well. 'Best on the floor. Saves picking it all up,' Matt said.

I got all choked up. 'Thanks, Mr Nagel. All this stuff...thank you!'

He shook his head. 'Least I could do, Lyla. You two have been in the thick of it.'

Matt said, 'It's going to get worse. Mum's on the warpath.'

'Tell me when,' I said. 'I'll leave you to it again.' I hoped his dad would stick around.

But Mr N had gone and I'd just filled the bowl to do the washing up when she hammered on the door.

I shut myself in my bedroom and turned my music up loud enough to drown her out when she started shouting.

I heard the front door slam after about half an hour. Once I was sure she'd gone I went to find Matt. He was sitting on the sofa looking like he'd just finished a full-on tug-of-war. It was hard to tell if he'd won or lost.

'You okay?'

'I'll live.'

'Here? Or Timaru?' I was reasonably interested in his answer.

He shut his eyes and slumped down into the cushions. 'According to Mum, I can stay here during the week and get the bus to Timaru weekends and holidays.'

She probably saw this as the perfect way to break her darling's rugby habit. 'Not happening?' I asked.

He grunted, then said, 'Dad's going to talk to your folks about me staying here.' There was almost a question in his voice.

I squashed down the temptation to pay him back for past torture. 'It's okay with me.'

He sat up a bit. 'Some schools are opening tomorrow.'

'Not ours?'

He shook his head. 'Nah. The word is that they're both wrecked. Totally munted.'

Gloom descended. I'd never moan about school again. I liked school, but I guess you don't get how important something is until it's not there. I wouldn't think about GG Block. It had been fully strengthened at the end of last century. It'd be okay, surely. 'Any word about when we can go back?'

But of course there wasn't. The new normal sucked – no clear answers, nothing to pin your life to. I made us hot chocolates loaded with sugar. I figured we needed it. I put Matt's in his hand – we didn't put full cups down in the new normal in case an aftershock rattled on through. 'What's your dad going to do? Is his office okay?'

'Yeah. Town's not so bad over there. He's going to bunk down in the tea room for now.' He buried his face in the choc mug. I got the message. Topic Parents = No Go.

Boys. They just didn't do talking. I wondered how Shona felt about her father turning up. He'd only kept in vague contact since her parents split when she was five. She often said she didn't really know him now. It was good that he'd joined them – you needed to know both parents loved you. I glanced at Matt. Maybe not the sort of love his mother dished out, though.

'Text your dad,' I said. 'Tell him to eat here tonight. He might as well. He's brought all the supplies.'

So that night we ate a dinner a proper chef wouldn't think much of. *These flavours just do not go together, Lyla. How could you think they did?* But my diners were properly appreciative and chowed down merrily on salad out of a bag, pasta bows and chilli followed by rainbow cake and lamingtons.

I managed not to listen to or view any news that evening. I didn't want to know how many people had died in the ruins of the cathedral.

Dad had good news for me. 'I found Ian at the hospital,' he said, giving me a hug. 'He was five minutes away from going home when I discovered him. Here. He wrote you a note. He hopes you won't mind the recycled card.'

I opened the envelope to read the card inside. A message to him from somebody called Clarry had been crossed out and another one written below it.

My very dear Lyla, I am so delighted to be able to thank you for saving my life. They tell me I'd be pushing up daisies by now were it not for your brave and prompt action. You are my hero.

Yours with deep appreciation,

Ian MacKenzie

I sniffed and looked at Dad. 'Is he really all right?'

He ruffled my hair. 'Sure is. His wife cried all over me when she found out I was related to you. Couldn't thank me enough for having the wit to father such a heroic child.'

I laughed, then leant against him. 'Is it still horrible? At the hospital, I mean?'

He stroked my back. 'It's not good, honey. This whole thing, it's just not good.' Then he took my shoulders and held me away so he could look me in the face. 'Tell me the truth. Are you happy for Matt to stay here for however long?'

I knew why he was asking – I'd moaned and complained about *idiot Matt Nagel* enough times before all this happened. I gave him a grin. 'I can't believe it myself, but yeah, I'm okay with it.'

Because right now idiot Matt Nagel was almost good to have around. He'd been great about getting Greer's computer. He'd helped with Leo and Henry. People did change, so maybe he was growing up.

I messaged Katie and Shona. *Matt N moving in. Lucky he doesn't snore.*

Katie: *You all still on lounge floor??? Why???*

Me: *Too scary to be by self in rockin-rollin bedroom.*

I stared at her message. It made me sad. Unless you were here in the city that never stood still, you didn't understand the comfort you got from all being together. My friends were drifting away.

I messaged Shona. *How's Greer?* The subtext being *when are you coming back to Chch?*

Sixteen

There was a message from Shona in the morning. *Greer heaps better. THANK YOU.*

Me: *Great. So when are you coming back?*

Shona: *Don't know.*

I could jump on a bus, trundle all the way down to Dunedin to visit her and Greer. How long would that take? I looked it up. Nearly six hours. I'd have to be away overnight. I couldn't face sitting on a bus for six hours, plus the thought of leaving my family for that long terrified me. What if another quake hit, another big one? I wouldn't know if they were okay.

I gave up on the visit idea.

Katie had messaged too. *Starting new school today. Nelson Girls. I HATE moving!!! Luv ya both.*

I sat staring at the screen for ages. All over the rest of the country, life was tootling on as normal. You got out of bed, jumped in the shower. If you wanted to wash your hair, you did. The water burbled its way down the drain without you giving it a thought. You could travel to work or school the same way every day without detouring when yet another road was closed for repairs.

There probably weren't any road cones or high-vis vests in any of those other cities – Christchurch had quite likely grabbed them all. We definitely had all the portaloos. Soldiers, cops, USAR teams, fire and ambo people – well, too bad for the rest of New Zealand.

The thing with disasters is you keep thinking they'll get better, that you'll wake up and everything will be back to how it used to be. But they don't get better, and you have to keep bracing for the next aftershock, the next news update.

I hated feeling useless. So much needed fixing. It didn't seem important enough to just shovel liquefaction and look after Leo and Henry. I took charge of the food situation. Each morning I set out for Dave and Myra's house with the boys, big and little varieties, tagging along too.

The conversation went something like this each day:

Myra: What'll we cook tomorrow, boys?

Henry: Spag bol!

Me and Matt: We're sick of spag bol. Think again.

Dave: You need veges, Henry. Got to grow those muscles.

Leo: We could have spag bol and veges.

Matt: Roast chicken and veges.

Me: Only if Myra tells me how to cook it.

Myra: Of course I will, dear. And I'll make an apple sponge pudding.

Leo wrote the list and Matt texted it to his father to buy at the one open supermarket on his way back to ours for dinner.

My mind was finding it hard to cope with the new Matt. He was brilliant and great company unless I strayed into a no-go area such as family break-ups or mothers. The little boys worshipped him – he was definitely the flavour of the month. Not that I cared. Well, to be truthful, I did. A bit. Which was so dumb, because it would have been pretty hellish trying to keep them calm and busy all by myself.

They wanted to do everything Matt was doing, so the three of them got busy every night peeling, chopping and stirring. I'd be doing something like browning meat for a casserole and I'd start wondering if I'd slipped into a parallel universe where Matt Nagel was almost a hero.

'What's with all the head-shaking?' he asked, suspicion in his voice.

'Onions. They get to me every time.'

A couple of days of continued saintliness from him and I finally figured out what it was all about. Matt Nagel was loving being part of a real family. Well, that was my theory and I thought it was a pretty good one.

His friends started coming over to hang out, and so did Millie, Jess and Joanne.

If the boys were with Natalie we all took off on our bikes searching for things to do. There were showers to be had, too – public ones at Pioneer Stadium. We didn't worry that it took ages to ride there; it helped fill in the day.

The Press published news about our schools, none of it good. Serious structural damage to both of them. The grounds of Shirley Boys' were awash with silt. Both principals said we wouldn't be back in either school, maybe for the rest of the year.

Joanne stabbed her finger on the article. 'They're looking at site-sharing. How will that work?'

Millie went pale. 'We might have to squash in with another class. There'll be no room and they'll hate us.'

Clancy – feral Clancy, who'd been on his bike since his dad found out about his driving stunt – said, 'Nah. It'll be one school in the morning and the other one swanning in at lunchtime when the first school packs it in for the day.'

Millie groaned. 'But which schools? And when can we go back? I just want to *know*. Nobody knows anything in this city anymore.'

There was good news on the second Saturday since the quake. All the rubble had been cleared from the cathedral. There were no bodies. Nobody had died there. Why does good news make you want to cry?

That evening Mum and Dad announced that they both had the day off on Thursday.

'About time,' I said. 'But what's so special about Thursday? Why not Wednesday? Or tomorrow?'

The only answer I got was two identical grins and, 'You'll work it out, darling,' from Mum.

Judging by the smug looks, everyone in that room over the age of eighteen was in on the joke – Myra, Dave, Robert, Blake, Matt's dad, Natalie and Don – all of them grinning away. Oh well, Thursday would turn up sooner or later and the mystery would be revealed.

I was pleased the parents were having a day off – finally. Both of them seemed kind of stretched thin. Their eyes were clouded, as if they'd seen too many bad things.

I worked out the Thursday thing during the night when an aftershock shook most of us awake.

'Thursday! Oh my god, it's my birthday! My fourteenth birthday!'

'Well done, honey,' Dad muttered. 'Now go back to sleep.'

How cool was that, though – I'd totally forgotten about my birthday but the parents had remembered. I think I slept the rest of the night with a grin on my face.

When you have a birthday in the middle of a disaster zone there's nowhere for people to go to buy you stuff, so I wasn't expecting presents. I'd forgotten snail mail was getting through again by now but my parents hadn't and when had a disaster ever stopped them? On Thursday morning there was a pile of parcels on the table.

'Happy birthday Lyla open your presents hurry up here's the scissors.' Henry took a breath at last.

But I didn't want to hurry. I grinned at him. 'Here, you can open this one.' It was small and it rattled. Lollies? Chocolates?

Mum slid into a chair beside me. 'We told the grands what to buy. Cross your fingers and hope their taste isn't too wild.'

The first parcel was the very trainers I'd told Nana Kiri to buy Mum. 'Okay?' Mum asked.

'Very okay!'

They'd done well with the three T-shirts, too. The bulkiest parcel was a new school backpack. I read the tag. 'It's from Ian and Beth. I don't know people called Ian and Beth.' Good taste, though – awesome in fact.

'You've met Ian,' Dad said. 'He says he's sorry he bled all over your other backpack.'

Earthquake Ian. I wanted to cry – he was all right. He really was alive and well.

'Can I have a lolly, Lyla? Please, please!'

Thank goodness for naggy kids. I swallowed the tears. 'One each, and only because it's my birthday.'

Leo said, 'You need birthday cards too, Lyla.' He slid a couple of folded pieces of paper across the table.

Henry leapt up and down, the lolly tin clutched in both hands. 'We made them ourselves.'

'Wow! They're brilliant. You sure you didn't buy them?' I hugged them – maybe they did still like me, just a bit.

Matt and his dad gave me a mirror for my bedroom. 'This is gorgeous! But how…where did you buy it?' Nothing was open – especially not the sort of place where you'd buy a mirror as stunning as this one.

'Let's just say it fell off a wall,' Matt said.

By which I figured it used to hang on a wall in his house, and had perhaps belonged to his mother. Too bad. I loved it. I was keeping it.

Myra and Dave arrived carrying the most delicious cake ever – chocolate, raspberry, icing and four candles. 'It's all we could find,' Dave said.

Birthday texts zapped in from Katie, Shona, Greer, Millie and Jess. Joanne turned up with a card she said her mum had stashed away. It said *Happy 40th birthday – life begins from here!* Joanne had crossed out the 0 and drawn a 1 in front of the 4.

I grinned at her. 'Thanks. I think!'

The day after my birthday, we got news of a huge earthquake and tsunami in Japan. Dinner that evening was a very sober meal. Nobody said much with Leo and Henry there, all wide-eyed and anxious and knowing something was wrong but not what it was. In the end, Don said, 'You know where Japan is?'

Nods from both kids, although Henry would probably point to Italy on a map of the world. 'Well,' said their dad, 'they've had an earthquake too. We're all feeling sad because we know how horrible that is.'

There was silence from both kids until Leo said, 'Can we still sleep here tonight, Dad? All of us in the lounge?'

Poor old Don – he so wanted to go back to his own

house, but he put his arms around his sons and said, 'Sure can, buddy.'

What was happening to the world? What catastrophe would hit next? Earthquakes sucked.

Seventeen

In the morning, once everyone including the little boys had disappeared for the day, Matt turned the TV on. The devastation in Japan was catastrophic. 'I'll never moan again about broken drains, dodgy water, no school,' I said.

Matt kept his eyes glued to the screen. 'Yeah, you will. But I know what you mean. Wish we could help.'

There it was again – that same old feeling of helplessness. I stood up. 'I'm going out. Want to come?'

He switched the images off. 'Might as well. Destination?'

'One plain, undecorated portaloo. We are going to transform it into a thing of beauty.' Or at least something more interesting than it was right now.

'Good call.' Matt took out his phone. 'I'll marshal the troops. Tell them to bring decorating materials.'

Millie and Jess helped me design and paint bright flowers winding their way over two sides of the loo then we found some real flowers still in their pots. Matt and a couple of his liquefaction gang boys painted something that looked vaguely like a shop window full of rugby and soccer balls. Feral Clancy bagsed the door. He was never going to make it as a graphic artist – the words of the *you know you're in Christchurch when*...jokes wobbled up and down across the door.

You know you're in Christchurch when a pile of students in your street is a Good Thing.

You know you're in Christchurch if you don't freak out when you see army tanks driving round town.

You know you're in Christchurch when you think a shower is da bomb!

And thus it was that when the parents and everyone else rocked on home that evening they all stopped to admire our artistic efforts.

Dad came in the door laughing. 'Love the joke about a game of Jenga only lasting three minutes in Christchurch.'

'Where did you get the plants?' Mum said. 'And the butterfly and gnome?'

Matt gave her his evil grin. 'We recycled the flowers from Mum's garden.'

His father winced and said, 'You're a braver man than I am.'

Millie and Jess had turned up with the gnome and butterfly. We didn't ask where they'd got them.

Our decorating efforts gave us all something cheerful to talk about at dinner even though Japan was heavy in our hearts. We didn't turn the telly on until the little boys were well asleep.

It was horrible. Our city and Japan – it was too much to take in. I went off to my bedroom to message Katie and Shona, but only Katie answered.

Me: *How's school?*

Katie: *It's ok. Everyone's kind. Want to be back at AGHS.*

Me: *Me too.*

Katie: *No idea when?*

Me: *Not this term and not at AGHS. Don't know where we'll be.*

Katie: *Sucks. You going to memorial service?*

Me: *????*

Katie: *You don't know?? Prince William's coming and all. Friday. It's a holiday.*

Me: *Been avoiding the news. Don't want to know latest death toll.*

We all went to the service on Friday the eighteenth of March, along with about a hundred thousand other people, most of us walking to the park so as not to clog up the roads in the city.

'It's a perfect day,' Myra said. 'A real scorcher.'

'The St John's people are going to be busy,' Dad said. He'd made us all – even Matt – bring hats, sunscreen and a water bottle each.

I caught comments from people we walked past. *Well, I think it's too soon. A memorial service when there are still bodies in the rubble.*

All these people. It's good. You don't feel so alone.

I wanna see Prince William!

Henry tugged on my hand. 'Will he have a crown on?'

'Don't think so, buddy. But they might give him a feather cloak to wear,' I said.

He gave me his serious look. 'It's called a korowai, Lyla. It's for important people. Ms Trenberth told us.'

'Hey, you! Good remembering.'

Leo leapt up and down, trying to see through the crowd. 'Everybody in the world is here! There won't be anywhere for us to sit. We need to hurry up, Dad.'

We weaved our way around groups already set up on the grass. Maybe this was a good idea – I felt the tight knot of tension unravelling its hold on me. We were safe out here in the open. It was easy to relax in the sunshine, listen to the music and chat to those around us. A guy with his arm in a heavy-duty sling grinned at Leo and Henry. 'This? I got clobbered by a stupid piece of verandah. I'm going to live in a shipping container from now on. No verandahs in those.'

The service started. The mayor welcomed everyone. 'Tihei mauri ora.' Let there be life – that was one meaning anyway. I was still thinking about that when the video of the central city started. It was in ruins, the streets full of rubble. I was glad when the speeches and the singing replaced it. At 12:51 we had the two minutes of silence and I was jolted straight back to when the quake had struck. Katie, Shona and me – cowering on ground that tried to throw us up back into the air. Buildings groaning and falling. Ian and blood. Eli and Selina – her baby could be born by now.

More speeches and more singing, and then it was over. 'I think I'm glad I came,' I muttered.

Mum gave my arm a squeeze. 'Me too.'

'I like that prince,' Myra said. 'A very impressive young man.'

'The korowai was nice but he should have a crown,' Henry said.

We were almost out of the park grounds when a small dog came racing up, barking its woolly head off. It leapt up at me and without thinking, I caught it – and got my face slobbered over. Then it clicked. 'Roger! Hi there, my old buddy.'

Mumma came panting up. 'I'm so sorry! He never does that. I don't know what's come over him – but he certainly likes you.'

I gave her a grin, but I was more interested in getting my face out of the way of his tongue. 'Hey, Roger, I get it. You're pleased to see me. And you're gorgeous, but a bit less of the slobber if you don't mind!'

She was gaping at me. 'How do you know his name? Oh! You're the girl who rescued him! Oh, how wonderful – and look, he remembers you. Clever Roger! Mumma's so proud of you!'

I set him back on the ground and he danced all round me, leaping up and – I swear – grinning at me. Leo and Henry got down on their haunches and tried to pat him. About one pat in every ten hit the mark.

'Mayhem,' Dave said. 'What's the story?'

Mumma told them her version, which didn't include her refusal to bash up her deck or how she didn't want to get me a towel. I filled in the gaps once they'd gone on their way.

'It's what you'd expect from a woman who refers to herself as *Mumma*,' Dad said.

Mum said, 'Well done, darling,' but she was eyeing me with that look that said *and what other deeds haven't you told me about?*

The days rolled on past, the aftershocks keeping us all tensed for the next one. Other kids returned to school, but we still didn't know when – and where – we'd get to go back.

I chucked my bike helmet down one afternoon when Matt and I got back from an excursion to look through the wire at the red zone of the central city. 'I hate seeing kids in uniform. Makes me so jealous I could scream.'

Matt looked up from his phone. 'Don't mind me. Scream away.'

I stomped off to my room. He wanted to be back in school too, even though he pretended he wasn't bothered.

It was well into March, a few days after the memorial service and with just two weeks left of the first term when we found out. The *when* was at the start of the new term. The *where* – Matt to Papanui High and me to Burnside High.

Katie: *You're going to Burnside? Seriously?? On the other side of town?*

Me: *Take me where the ground don't dance, sister. It'll be ok. Special buses. Start at lunchtime. Finish 5ish. Just good to be back at school. Any school.*

Katie: *Burnside's huge. But hey, you'll meet boys!!*

Me: *I wish. They leave. We arrive.*

There was a meeting for parents and girls at Burnside High on the Friday before we started the new arrangement on Monday. We'd be able to ask about how it was all going to work.

Joanne, Millie, Jess and I met up in the morning at Joanne's house to talk about it.

'Those kids are going to hate us,' Millie said, her eyes wide and worried. 'I'd hate it. I mean, they're going to have to get up so early because of us. I'm not even conscious at eight in the morning.'

'I'm terrified of getting lost. There's about three thousand kids at that school,' Jess said.

Joanne and I made the soothing comments – it wouldn't help to admit we were slightly nervous ourselves. It was harder for the Year Nines like Millie and Jess – they'd only had two weeks of high school when our world shook itself to pieces. Not enough time to get used to anything.

They and their parents were waiting for us outside the hall. We all went in together, bracing ourselves for news of who was missing, who wouldn't be coming back.

'There's Amy!' Jess shrieked.

'Ananta! Over here!' Millie ran and threw her arms around a girl standing close to her dad and looking lost.

It was going to be okay. It was so unbelievably good to see familiar faces again. All my teachers were there, every single one of them.

Lots of tears, lots of hugging. It felt like we were a school again. It almost didn't matter that we were far away from our own buildings, our own grounds – we were here in this borrowed space with our own teachers, our own classmates. We were still Avonside Girls' High School.

Although I'd told Millie the Burnside kids would be fine with us being there, I'd worried that we'd feel like interlopers, that they'd be annoyed at having their lives thrown into chaos. I should have known better. They welcomed us and made us feel at home.

I said goodbye to Joanne at the end of the evening. 'It's not going to be so bad.'

'Yep. Just good to be going back. Weird to miss it so much.'

'Tell me about it!'

There was a message from Shona when I got home. *Moving to Whangarei. Mum totally freaked by quakes. Sad. Don't want to go.*

Not coming back? Never? I put my head down on my desk and howled. I needed my friends. Friends were solid – the earth could go mad, but you could depend on your friends.

And now I couldn't.

Another tremor shook the house. I stayed where I was – no point in moving for anything less than a four. But my heart wasn't so good at working out what was a four and what wasn't. It sped up to full revs at the slightest excuse.

Hateful, vile, foul, *disgusting* bloody earthquakes.

Eighteen

We settled into our new school routine. The periods were shorter to fit the shorter day. My part-time job looking after Leo and Henry in the afternoon didn't fit with when I got home from school. Goodbye, pocket money.

Being able to go to school again helped. It felt like normal wasn't so far away. I was glad to have assignments to think about and other things besides disaster to fill my head with.

The city kept changing. In the morning the bus would go past a row of shops with gaping holes where the entire front walls had fallen off. In the afternoon, there'd be no shops, just a patch of bare earth. Bulldozers, cranes, machinery – the city was alive with them.

The days shortened as we got into winter. When school finished for the day we boarded our buses in the dark and travelled home in the dark.

In school, nobody took much notice of an aftershock below four. All the teachers were pretty Zen about them.

But we had a relief teacher one day for Social Studies when there was a three point five. Mr Jenks leapt to his feet, yelling his head off. 'Forswear that, you foul fiend! Fie upon you! Flee and never trouble us again.' Then he sat down again as if nothing had happened. 'Do continue with your work, young ladies.'

A stunned silence before our entire class shrieked with laughter.

He lifted his head from his book and grinned. 'Yes. Well.'

You know you're in Christchurch when your teacher goes nuts.

Things at home were just about back to normal, with only my family plus Matt in the house. Leo and Henry had calmed down enough to sleep in their own place.

The Chan family were going to rent Mrs Malone's house, even though the front wall was propped up with lengths of timber. 'Why isn't Mrs M coming back?' I asked. She wouldn't want to abandon her garden – she was always out in it.

'The quakes have shaken her confidence,' Mum said. 'She doesn't want to live by herself anymore. She's settled in with her son's family and taken over their garden.'

I'd miss her, but it'd be good to have the Chans back in the street. 'What about Prof? Have you heard from him?'

'Didn't you notice?' Mum asked. 'His house has been red-stickered. He's staying in Wanaka until things settle down a bit.'

We'd stopped sleeping on the lounge floor when Natalie and Co moved back home. Our mattresses went back on the beds and everyone returned to their own rooms.

The window in Blake's room got mended and Matt moved in with him, which Blake didn't seem to mind.

I shut my door, as far as it would go. I had my very own space again with no kids in the house to come bashing on the door. I didn't put my new mirror on the wall. Along with anything heavy, like my hair dryer and the lava lamp Shona had found in an op shop, the mirror stayed on the floor.

I liked being by myself, I really did – and if I told myself that enough I'd believe it in the end. It took me a week to get used to being alone in the darkness. Stupid foul fiend earthquakes – I was handling them.

But it doesn't pay to get too pleased with yourself when you live in a shaky city. Every time an aftershock jerked me awake, what did I do? I trotted off to sleep on the floor in the parents' room, that's what I did.

The days rolled on by, punctuated by aftershocks but some good happenings as well. A totally awesome happening was our whole class getting goody bags from a school in the North Island. The kids from Hastings Girls' High had fundraised and sent us a whole bunch of stuff.

We fell on those bags. Pencils, pens, felt pens, stationery, girly stuff. Just knowing other people were still thinking of us, still wanting to help – that was huge. I carefully packed it all up, took it home and arranged it on my bedroom floor where a) it couldn't fall b) I could see it and c) nobody would walk on it. Whenever I used a pen or a sheet of pretty writing paper I made sure to put everything back in its place.

That corner turned into my go-to place when I was feeling low, fed up or just vaguely annoyed with life. All that stuff reminded me that other people did care. They couldn't be here in my city, but they hadn't forgotten us.

We didn't know what was going to happen with our house. Its fate was the same old Christchurch story – nothing was certain and things kept changing. First of all the inspectors said our house would be fixed. Then another lot of men with clipboards said it couldn't be. Next we were told the ground was too unstable and we couldn't rebuild even if our house had to be bulldozed.

The parents spent hours on the phone to officialdom, but in the end gave up. 'We'll live in it till they pull it down round our ears,' Dad said.

Fine by me. The floor sloped, none of the doors would shut properly and there were gaps in some of the corners. But we were lucky: we had a house that kept us dry and reasonably warm. The drains got fixed, the water flowed from the taps – yep, we were one of the lucky families in a city where people were living in garages and tents with nowhere else to go when winter properly hit.

Veronica in my class had moved five times already since February and she said they'd have to move again before the end of June. Louisa's house had a tarpaulin instead of a side wall; they wanted to move out but rental places were almost impossible to find. Becky, Freya, Aimee and Christie's houses were wrecked and they hadn't been able to save anything.

I went to school on Monday of the third week in June with everything ticking along nicely. I still missed Katie and Shona, but I now had earthquake friends like Matt, Joanne, Freya, Millie and Jess. Some days, I even added Feral Clancy to my list.

We were in our first lesson for the day and all was well until it wasn't. The room rattled and shook, desks skidded around on the floor. Mrs D yelled, 'Drop, cover, hold!' but we'd already all dived under our desks.

Somebody near me was crying. Veronica. As if she hadn't had enough drama already this year. Mr Jenks and his hissy fit flicked across my memory. I yelled, 'Forswear, foul fiend! Fie upon you! Flee and never trouble us again.'

Veronica hiccupped; Freya and a couple of others laughed. The siren was going – evacuation. Out we trooped onto the sports field. 'A five. That was at least a five.'

Some of the guesses were wild – nine point two, eight point seven. No way.

We found out later that it was a five point five.

The school had to be closed for inspection to

make sure it wasn't going to collapse on our heads. We went home.

Natalie, you want me to collect the boys?

Got them thanx. Glad yr ok.

I walked slowly from the bus stop. Bloody ground – why couldn't it just stay in one place? Who needed earth that upped and bounced around just for the fun of it? Not me.

I turned the corner before our place and, oh joy, Mrs Nagel's car was parked across the gutter.

I can do this. I can be polite. I wished she hadn't chosen an earthquake day to visit – my nerves were still rattling and my heart grabbed any old excuse to do the pile-driver drum riff.

I shoved the front door open, dropped my bag, stuck a smile on my face and walked into the lounge. 'Hi, Matt. Hello, Mrs Nagel, would you like…'

'Lyla Sherwin, can't you see I'm speaking to my son? Where are your manners? Leave us alone. Go on. Get out.'

Matt held his head. 'Mum! You can't…jeez!'

Rage, red hot and burning, filled every atom of me. Force ten on the quake scale. I jammed one fist on my hip and pointed at the door. 'This is *my* house, not yours. *You* get out. Right now. *Leave!*'

Mrs Nagel sat there, going red and doing the stranded fish gasp, then heaved herself up. 'Come on, Matthew. We'll leave this young *lady* in charge of *her* house.'

Matt kept his butt firmly in his chair. 'Goodbye, Mum.'

'The door's that way.' I took a massive stride towards her. I was mad enough to grab her.

She gave me a snooty look. I glared; she caved and scuttled around me.

I didn't move till we heard her car take off with the engine revving.

The adrenalin faded. I looked at Matt. 'Sorry.'

'She deserved it.' Short, sharp, didn't want to talk about it.

Fine.

The house shook, the earth rumbled, I fell down, Matt got thrown from the chair. We hunkered down on the floor, turtle style. This felt worse than the earlier quake. My heart felt as if any minute now I'd be spewing it up on the carpet. I couldn't stand it, couldn't take any more.

But you have to, just like you have to pick up the stuff from the pantry, put back the contents of the fridge and clean up the spills.

And text the parents and Blake. *I'm ok. You?*

They were all good, but Mum and Dad would be working late. Damage in the city. The emergency room busy with the injured.

We gathered the neighbours for a communal meal. That night, Leo, Henry and their parents slept on our lounge floor with Matt, my family and the Chans. I was so glad to be one of a crowd.

Aftershocks shuddered through all night long.

But it turned out that nature *still* hadn't finished with my city.

Nineteen

We got snow. In the July holidays the weather turned bitter and the snow powered down.

Matt stood at the window. 'We need a snowman. Can't waste the white stuff.'

'I'll summon the workforce.' I reached for my phone.

Snowman planning meeting at ours, 11am sharp! Bring your best techniques and ideas!!

Five minutes before the hour our lounge was busting at its cracked seams with snowman-construction experts. Millie, Jess, most of the kids from our liquefaction brigade. Henry and Leo bouncing out of their skins. Joanne was there with her brother. Feral Clancy lay flat on the floor.

We took several hours to build that sucker – it must have been the hugest snowman in the city. A combination of big and little boys had even managed to set another small one up on top of the portaloo.

Anyway, while we were playing in the snow there were officials all over the country scratching their heads and worrying about how to host the seventh Rugby World Cup when one of the key venues had gone and made itself unusable.

As the snow melted Matt talked about rugby non-stop. Fine by me. It helped keep the deaths out of my head. A hundred and eighty-five. That's how many people had died in the February quake. Bring on the rugby.

Matt planned his campaign. He intended to watch every All Blacks' game from the fanzone in Hagley Park where, he told me several times, there would be huge screens and lots of atmosphere just like at a real game. 'You can tag along too, if you like,' he said.

'Sure.' For some of them, anyway. The Aussie–NZ games – I intended to be where I could watch and cheer and bite my nails. I wanted to go to the New Zealand versus Tonga opening game too.

I couldn't wait. The idea of being part of a crowd that had nothing to do with earthquakes – brilliant. The Tonga game kicked off at eight-thirty in the evening, so I had plenty of time to get home from school and to the park fanzone before kick-off.

Matt's rugby fever infected our whole neighbourhood. Imelda Chan bossed her family into coming. You couldn't have stopped Leo and Henry with a force five-point-five quake. Myra and Dave, Blake, Mum and Dad, Matt's dad, Millie, Jess, Joanne and their families, Feral Clancy – all of us made plans. How to get there and what to take.

Something to look forward to – great. But then Matt's school reopened on its own site in September and his day went back to normal and just like that, my life felt a lot harder. And that set off the guilts. So many others were struggling with real problems – injuries, deaths of loved ones, homelessness. All I had to do was go to school at a weird time. *Get a grip, Lyla Sherwin.*

It didn't make a blind bit of difference to how I felt. Swearing helped, but not for more than a few seconds. I simply hadn't understood the solidarity I'd got from him having to deal with the same school upset as I did. Who'd have thought? Matt Nagel, support buddy? But being sarcastic didn't help either.

So I went to watch the rugby. I cheered and groaned and lost myself in the excitement of each game. It was good. I felt resilient.

The All Blacks got into the quarter-finals, then the semis and then the final. We'd play France in Auckland at Eden Park at the end of the October holidays.

The day arrived. We hit the fanzone. Henry kept leaping around, questions pouring out. 'Will we win, Matt? We will, won't we? The score's gunna be us 72 and France nil.'

Leo looked nervous. Imelda worked on looking cool – not easy when your face is painted solid black with a silver fern across the chin.

The All Blacks won 8–7 but I reckon I wasn't the only one whose heart nearly stopped a thousand times over during those eighty minutes. Tense! There needs to be a force nine word for the tension we all felt. And the roar when the final whistle went was a force ten.

We walked home on a high.

The win and the whole atmospheric excitement made going back to school at the wrong time of the day okay. Life went on. Fun still happened, and we had the opening of the start-up mall to look forward to at the end of October – shops in shipping containers. It felt like the central city was beginning to come alive again.

But in the days between the rugby ending and the start-up mall opening, Mr Nagel found a place to rent and Matt moved out. 'See ya round, Lyla S.'

I lifted a hand in farewell. He high-fived me. I couldn't believe how much I didn't want him to go. Who could I talk to now? Of course Matt didn't do talk, but he'd been there through the worst of it. In his own weird way he'd been kind. If he did get to be an All Black, I'd go and watch him play.

Having him around had helped. Like, I could tell he was freaked out too when an aftershock happened. Meals, dishes, washing, kid-minding – he'd helped with all of it. Matt Before Quake was horrible. Matt Post Quake was okay. And now he wasn't here, and it sucked.

Twenty

Fate had more to chuck into the mix before October ended. There was news about GG Block at my old school. It was being torn down.

I suddenly didn't feel like going to the mall opening. Big deal – shops again. Who cared? Not me.

As it turned out, I should have sucked it up and gone to the stupid opening of the dumb mall. Not going gave the parents the opportunity to ask Probing Questions. 'How are you feeling, Lyla?'

'Fine. Don't keep hassling me.'

'Is school going okay? How are you coping with the homework?'

'No problemo, I get it done in the mornings.'

'How are you coping without Katie and Shona around?'

'I miss them, but Joanne, Freya and I hang out now.'

'Are you as close to them as you are to Katie and Shona?'

'Oh for crying down the broken chimney! Stop hassling me!'

They were always watching me, checking my mood temperature. It drove me nuts. I was fine. If sometimes I felt like I was wading through thigh-deep liquefaction, so what? I wouldn't be the only one in the city who wasn't exactly a box of fluffies right now.

The liquefaction hit the fan thanks to Mrs Ghastly Nagel. She rang the landline at ten one Tuesday evening. Mum snatched it up, all of us thinking *Late call. What's happened? Who's sick/injured/in hospital?* Mum automatically hit the speaker button – best to do that. It avoids the need to repeat rotten news.

The voice of the Queen of Ghastliness erupted. 'Clemmie, I want you to go and get some things from the house. I've got a list. You'll need to write it down.'

Mum took a deep breath, or maybe two. Mrs N said, 'Clemmie? Are you ready?'

I never liked to be on the receiving end of Mum's voice when it went deadly calm and icy cold. 'Candace, I am not going near your house. It's red-stickered and very unstable. Goodbye.'

Then the Queen of Horrible said, 'I should have guessed you'd refuse to help me. And as for your daughter's egregious behaviour...'

What?

But yay for my mother. In a voice colder than the July snowstorm, she said, 'And what about your part in this *egregious* behaviour, Candace? What did you do to make my daughter angry enough to lose her temper?'

Apparently Mrs N didn't want to go into her own

eg-whatever behaviour. We heard her splutter before the line went dead.

Mum plonked down the receiver. 'Bloody woman. What happened, Lyla?'

So I had to tell her the whole gory story of me ordering the woman out. Mum winced – at Mrs N, not me. 'Unbelievable. Matt's not got it easy with a mother like her.'

I shook my head and kept it down to hide the tears just waiting to spill over and alert the parents that I was a tad shaky.

But apparently parents were meant to be looking out for signs of stress in their kids and I got even more attention focused on my 'well-being'.

I held it together, mainly by talking to Joanne and Freya about how other people were coping. Joanne said her grandmother took a friend from New Plymouth to look at the Red Zone. They peered through the wire fence at the cathedral and her grandmother cried.

Freya's mother wouldn't go into a supermarket. 'She's terrified of things falling on her.'

I told them about Myra's friend Elaine who went to Auckland for a break. 'She's wanted to go up the Sky Tower forever. But Myra said when she got there she freaked out. Tall building. Lifts. No way.'

We didn't talk about ourselves and we didn't talk about the demolition of our school. I didn't want to discover they were as jumpy as I was. We needed each other to be okay. I could keep on going if everyone around me just got on with it.

The wheels fell off the trolley in the middle of November. All I did was stomp in after school and kick the door harder than usual to get it shut.

'How was school, Lyla?' Mum asked, her gimlet eyes boring into me.

Leave me alone. I dumped my bag. 'It was okay. Not brilliant – it's not the same without Katie and Shona. And I can't believe I'm saying this, but I kind of miss having Matt around.' *Pick up on the decoy topic, Mum. Let's talk about Matt. Or Shona and Katie.*

Why did I think that would work?

'I've made a counselling appointment for you for Friday.' She plonked a hand on my shoulder. 'No arguments, Lyla.'

'Mum! I don't need counselling!' I got out of there before I exploded all over the kitchen.

I just one hundred per cent knew the parents would be exchanging one of their worried-over-Lyla looks. Well, let them. I was fine. I was handling it. I was one of the lucky ones – somewhere to live, parents who cared (a bit too much), new friends. I wouldn't be the only one to think *earthquake* when I heard the roar of a truck engine or a plane. It wouldn't be just my heart taking off like a racehorse, because I wasn't the only jumpy one in the city.

I absolutely was not going to sit down with a counsellor, unless they could stop the aftershocks and magic the city back to whole again. Like that was going to happen. Neither of the parents mentioned the counselling appointment all week, and I didn't remind them.

On Friday, Dad was waiting for me after school. He opened the car door. 'Hop in, Lyla.'

I got in. It was nice to be picked up from school, but unusual enough to make me suspicious. 'Where are we going?'

'Counselling.'

Oh. Hard to believe, but I'd forgotten. 'If it's not in a single-storey building I'm not getting out of this car.'

She was in a single-storey office in Riccarton, where every business that used to be in a high-rise in town seemed to have relocated to.

When Dad stopped the car he said, 'It's hard living here now, hon. Take all the help you can get. Clemmie and I – both of us have regular counselling.'

He leant over to give me a hug. 'You're a great kid. But your mum and I suspect you're struggling more than you realise.'

Am not struggling.

The counsellor said to call her Cilla. Her grey hair might have been tidy when she'd arrived at work, but by the looks of things she'd dragged her hands through it more than a few times since then.

It took her about three point five minutes to crack me open. Utter humiliation for an entire hour. I howled and hiccupped and bellowed – I was my own personal earthquake.

I went through all the tissues she had left in the box on her desk. I know she asked me questions, because each time she did I howled a whole new gush of disgusting wetness.

Exhausting. By the end of the fifty minutes, I couldn't sit up straight.

Dad came in. Through the fog, I heard *battle fatigue* and *complete break somewhere safe.*

If I'd had any energy left I'd have had hysterics – there wasn't anywhere safe. Nowhere. Nothing was ever going to be safe again.

Twenty-one

The very next day I was on a plane, winging my way across the Tasman to Brisbane where my grandparents would be waiting for me.

'Don't worry about school,' the parents told me. 'We'll sort it out. Think of this as sick leave.'

Whatever. Too hard to think. I didn't even know what I thought about being parcelled up and posted to another country for however long it took to cure me of bursting into tears anytime anyone looked at me.

Wretched counsellor. I was fine until she got stuck into me.

I slept. We landed in Brisbane. Somehow I found the strength to get myself off the plane. The temperature in the airbridge was warm. It was late in the evening. The day at home had been colder than this. Warm was nice.

Grandy and Nana Lilith hugged me, collected my bag, stowed me in their car and didn't bother me with talk. I was grateful. I slept again, only waking up when

Nana Lilith put her arm around my shoulders. 'Come along, sweet girl.'

I unscrambled myself from the car. Even in the darkness I could tell we weren't anywhere near their Sunshine Coast apartment. 'What? Where?'

I was looking at a house raised above the ground but not in a scary way. It had big windows and wide verandahs. It looked friendly.

'We thought you'd feel safer away from tall buildings,' Grandy said. 'We'll stay here in the country for a week and then we'll decide what to do.'

They tucked me into bed in a room with a ceiling fan. When I woke up the sun was hot.

The grandparents had food plus a heap of tourist brochures spread out on the table. 'We've eaten,' Nana said. 'Help yourself.'

I made a sandwich – tomato, cheese, ham and pickle. Then I made another one. 'This is so good.' I hadn't relished my food like this for months. Maybe this holiday – sick leave – wasn't such a stupid idea after all.

'Where are we?' In the middle of nowhere, by the look of it. All I could see was farmland and a few houses in the distance.

'We're in the Lockyer Valley.' Grandy slid a map across the table. 'See? Here.' He pointed a pen at a spot, then moved it to a circle labelled *Laidley*. 'That's our nearest town. We'll go there in a minute to stock up on food.'

I felt myself relaxing as we tootled along country roads into Laidley. I felt safe, this place felt safe.

Even when we got back and I noticed some of the trees near the house had trunks blackened by bushfires, I didn't panic. Nana saw me looking at them. 'I don't think we need to worry about fires right now.' She pointed at the sky, where thunderous rainclouds were already drenching the far hills.

The storm reached us not long after. I ran outside onto the lawn, whirling and dancing in the sluicing rain. The grandparents laughed and videoed me. 'Put that on Facebook and you're dead!'

So everything was going brilliantly, even when a couple of days later Grandy announced we were going to a lake in search of fauna. I thought about it for half a second. Snakes, scorpions, poisonous spiders – whatever. I'd survived thousands of earthquakes. A bit of wildlife wasn't going to faze me.

We left early because my grandparents didn't know how to lie in bed and laze in the mornings, so I was still mostly asleep when we got to the lake.

'Where's the fauna?' I couldn't see anything flying, running or swimming. 'It's too early. All sensible fauna is still tucked up and snoring.'

Grandy pointed at the middle of the lake. 'How about that?'

'It's a swan, Grandy. Swans don't come under the heading of exotic fauna.' Actually, it was a pretty weird-looking swan. I glanced at the grandparents. They grinned back at me – the sort of grin that said they knew something I didn't.

'What?' I took another look at the fauna. 'Hey! That swan's a pelican!' I instantly forgave them for the early morning. A pelican! How cool was that!

Nana started walking. 'I reckon that clump of white birds down the end on the shore are probably pelicans too. Worth a look, anyway.'

It wasn't the most picturesque walk I've ever been on. We had to walk down a muddy track dodging thigh-high weeds but not to worry – we were on a pelican hunt.

'Yep! Pelicans!' A whole bunch of them – twenty at least. Every now and then one of them would tip his head back and clack his beak in a huge yawn. Go, pelicans!

We couldn't get really close because a sludgy stream got in the way, but I didn't mind. It was just fun standing there watching them do nothing much – until I got to the stage of wishing they'd get active. Time to go. I turned around. The grandparents were halfway back to the car. Between me and them was the wasteland of weeds. Snakes lived in undergrowth like that. Poisonous spiders, scorpions and stonking great lizards. Huh! Wildlife I could handle.

I got back to the grandparents with a huge grin on my face. 'Fantastic fauna, Grandy. What else have you got?'

'Coffee in town,' Nana said. 'Then we'd better go back and put our muddy clothes in the wash.'

Yeah. We were a bit grubby. Quite grubby, actually, but when we got back to the house there would be running water in the shower and a washing machine that worked.

The coffee, when we found a place that was open, was good and so was my hot chocolate and the croissants with apricot jam. We drank, ate and drove back to our house before the sun was properly out of bed. But that was my grandparents – got to be up and doing. Couldn't lie in bed half the day, especially not when there was mud to be tramped through and pelicans to be found.

Grandy shoved our grubby gear into the washing machine and set it going. I scrubbed the mud of Australia off my shoes and propped them up on the verandah to dry in the sun. Give me mud over liquefaction sludge any old day of the week.

'How does the idea of a proper breakfast appeal?' Nana asked.

'Eggs? Bacon? Tomatoes?' Oh yes, that appealed all right.

She laughed and told me to bring the eggs.

I grabbed them out of the fridge and the house started to shake. No! I dropped to the floor, scrabbled my way under the table and cowered, shaking harder than the house could ever do.

Grandy appeared beside me. His arm was warm across my quivering back. 'Lyla – honey girl, it's okay. It's not an earthquake. It's the washing machine.'

I shook my head. 'Stay down. Stay under cover. Please, Grandy – don't die. Don't let Nana die.'

But all he did was go on about washing machines. The shaking stopped. Nana Lilith's voice came from somewhere above me. 'I've turned it off, Lyla. It's okay. Come on out.'

Together they hauled me to my feet. I was so ashamed. 'Sorry. I've never freaked out like that before. Not even for the big ones.'

They sat me down on the sofa. 'Listen, darling,' Grandy said, 'this place is on stilts. It probably shakes in a high wind too.' He got up. 'I'll make you a drink. Lots of sugar in it for shock.'

I hid my head in my hands. 'I feel so stupid. I've never been like this at home.'

Nana put her arm around me. 'Darling girl – think for a moment. At home you're always expecting the next quake. It doesn't surprise you. But here you weren't expecting the house to start shaking.'

It sounded logical, except that she didn't know how unpredictable the world could be. She didn't know how things could change in seconds and then never settle down.

I was so tired. I stood up and walked to the window. I should have brought a tent. I could sleep on the lawn and it wouldn't matter if the ground went nuts.

There was a kookaburra on the power line and wallabies hopping around under the trees. I wanted to feel excited about seeing them, but I just felt tired.

The grandparents put me to bed and I slept until the heat of the afternoon woke me. I was hungry. That had to be good. I wouldn't be hungry if I was dying.

Grandy gave me a hug when I tottered from the bedroom. 'Food for you on the table, Lyla. You want water, tea or fruit juice?'

'Juice, thanks. Hey, what's with the packed bags?'

Their cases waited by the door along with a box of groceries. 'And where's Nana?'

Grandy pulled out a chair for me. 'Eat. We're going back to Brisbane. We're going to stay in the house of some friends – single-storey. They're going away, so it'll just be us. And their dog.'

I started piling stuff into a bread roll. 'But why? I mean, here's great.' But I knew. You couldn't go around having full-blown meltdowns and expect your grandparents to ignore it.

'Your nana is organising counselling for you. Can't do it from here. No internet.'

I dropped my head into my hands. 'I don't want to go to counselling. Bloody counselling made Mum and Dad send me over here.'

He came and sat across the table from me. 'Well, honey, I look at it this way. When I was working, if I got a piece of equipment that had a massive blowout, then a few days later it had another one – I figured I'd better get the whole thing overhauled.'

'I'm not a machine.'

May as well not have said anything, because he kept on with the gosh-awful analogy. 'Of course, I always had a choice – fix it or keep on using it till it completely wrecked itself.'

I pushed my plate of untouched lunch away. 'Grandy, I don't want to go to counselling. You have to go back into all that stuff. And I don't want to. It's too scary.'

I'd never noticed what a kind face my grandfather had. He was an expert at looking kind, sympathetic and determined all at the same time. 'It's not so hot being in your head right now, though, is it? And how are you going to live the rest of your life if you can't go up in a lift or cope with the heap of other things that might trigger the panic?' He slid the plate back to me. 'Eat up. Nana will have things organised. She's got contacts in the counselling world.'

I ate, hoping she wouldn't be able to get me an appointment before I was due to go home. Waiting lists and all that.

Twenty-two

We were just coming into Brisbane when Nana Lilith's phone went. It might be one of their friends. It might be... But no, what I was hearing wasn't one side of a friend-type conversation.

'Yes, this is Lilith Sherwin. Oh, that's wonderful. Tonight at six? Thank you so much. It's very kind of you.'

There was no escape. The counsellor was going to stay late as a special favour to Nana.

Great.

We went to the friends' place. They practically fell on us, they were so grateful – their dog-sitter had had a last-minute crisis and cancelled. While they raved to the grandparents I made friends with the dog.

'What's her name?' I asked.

The man dropped to his haunches to rub the dog's ears. 'This is our Lolly. You're gorgeous, aren't you, girl?'

Lolly was a fine-boned Doberman, shiny black. She stared in disbelief when the man jumped up, said,

'Bye, Lolly. See you in a week,' and strode out the door with the suitcases.

I put my arms around her. 'It's okay, Lolly. We'll look after you.' I rubbed her ears and I reckon if she'd been a cat she'd have purred.

I played with that dog for the rest of the afternoon. We went for a walk around the neighbourhood and I didn't once worry about snakes or shakes. I was cured. All I needed was a dog.

The grandparents had other ideas. I had to leave Lolly behind when Nana drove me to the appointment. I didn't moan, I knew how to be polite.

I can do this. I've lived through thousands of earthquakes. I can survive one lousy counselling session.

Dr James Moran was ancient. He looked like a wild man from the bush. He greeted me with a firm handshake and a casual grin. 'So, young Lyla – I'm told you're not a fan of counselling.'

Great intro, Dr James. I gave him a weak smile. 'I'm grateful you could fit me in. It's very kind of you.'

'Ooh,' he said. 'Liar liar pants on fire! You're hating every moment.'

What sort of doctor was he? And who was dumb enough to give him those fancy-looking certificates on the wall?

He laughed and waved me to a chair. 'Have a seat. That's the girl. Now, how about you say what you're really feeling about being here?'

I shook my head. 'You don't want to know. The grandparents would be mortified.'

He settled back in his chair and stuck his feet on the coffee table between us. 'I do want to know, and they're not here. So let fly.'

Really? Well, he asked for it. 'I don't want to go back and re-live all that stuff by talking about it. I'm okay if I just keep going. If I don't think about it I can cope.'

I was surprised when he nodded. 'Yes, your gran told me you've been brilliant. A stalwart of the street, and particularly a life-saver for your immediate neighbour and her children.'

Now he was just sitting there looking at me. 'What?'

'Let's not talk about the quakes. We'll talk about right now. Talk about what it's like being in Lyla's body at this moment.'

I shook my head. 'I don't want to be here.'

That earned me a *good girl*, but then he said, 'Tell me what that feels like.'

'Bad. It feels bad.'

'What sort of bad?'

I so didn't want to. 'It's hard to breathe. I can't sit up straight.' I was trying not to start howling all over his stupid office.

'What else?' asked my tormentor.

The tears started. Oh please, not another slushy session. He pushed over a box of tissues and just sat there till I calmed down enough for him to fire more questions at me.

'Tell me what that was all about.'

'I don't know. I just don't know.' I was so tired. I wanted to be left alone. I wanted to sleep with Lolly the Doberman curled up on the bed beside me.

It seemed I'd said that out loud. He said, 'What would that feel like? To be in bed with the dog beside you?'

I sighed. 'Safe. It would feel safe, like nothing bad could happen.'

'Your world hasn't felt like that for a long time now?'

'No.' Such a dumb question.

'Tell me about that.'

'Do I have to?' Apparently I did have to. 'I've been fine. I know what to do when a quake hits. I'm the one who keeps calm. Mum and Dad made me go to counselling and that's what started all this horrible stuff.'

I hoped he'd defend counselling and leave me alone. No such luck. 'How have you been feeling these last months?'

I shrugged. 'It's hard. You've no idea what it's like living in a broken city – always waiting for the next aftershock.'

'No, I haven't. You're quite right. So tell me what that's like.'

Okay, I walked right into that. 'It's crap. Everybody's jumpy. We all laugh and crack jokes, but underneath it all we're like the ground – shaky.'

'What about you? Are you jumpy even though you laugh and crack jokes? Do you feel shaky and unstable? Do you feel that nothing in your life is safe or dependable any longer?'

I could only nod. 'There's no safe place. Not anymore.' I lifted my head to look him straight in the eye. 'And there never will be ever again.'

'No,' he said. 'The world isn't a safe place. How about we talk about ways you can live with that?'

'If you want.' *Whatever. Just let me out of here.*

He didn't say anything, and when I looked up he was sitting there in his stupid chair with his stupid feet up on the stupid coffee table staring at me.

'What?'

'Lyla, this session isn't about what *I* want. I'm not the one who has to go back home to a place where I'm always braced for the next quake, where I never feel safe, where others are depending on me to be strong.'

'All *right!* Tell me how to live with it.' He wouldn't be able to, I knew that right down to my bones.

'I can't cure you...'

Ha! I knew counselling was useless, but at least he was honest. I went to get up, but plopped down again when he said, 'What I can do is help you understand why you feel crap and give you a few things to help you live more peacefully in your unstable world.'

'Does that mean I don't have to talk about what it was like? I don't have to remember it all over again?'

'No. Later you might find it helpful to do that, but not right now.'

I breathed out, relaxing for the first time in months. 'Okay. That sounds good. I'd like that.'

That earned me a grin and another *good girl.* He talked about how the quakes were hard to deal with because they were ongoing. 'It's like having a bad burn that keeps on getting scorched. It's always there and you're always braced for the next shock. That means that anything can set off the amygdala part of your brain, that's the bit that's responsible for memory, emotions and survival instincts. If something triggers it, it goes into the fight-or-flight response. Heart racing, breathing difficult, sick feeling.'

'You mean it's natural to get…like that when a plane goes over? Or there's a truck out on the road?' I was so ashamed of panicking over nothing.

'Indeed it is, so you need to know how to take care of yourself. We'll look at how to do that next time.' He sat up and planted his feet on the floor. 'What's happening with you is what's sometimes called an amygdala hijack. I'll send Lilith a link. She says you're not short on brains, so jump online and read up on it. You'll find it'll help to know what you're experiencing is pretty common and that it's treatable.'

I got back to find an email from Mum. After the *how are you darling* bit there were newsy bits. The Jaffries' house had been demolished. The Chans' place would be next, then Prof's and lastly the Nagels'. *Candace Nagel rang again to tell us to retrieve her list of stuff. Hope she doesn't turn up to do it herself. Wouldn't be a good look to whip the handcuffs on her. Tempting, though!*

So. My street would be different when I got home from how it was when I left. The old amygdala went into orbit. I sat on the couch with Lolly, holding her and stroking her till my heart rate settled.

If I was losing it, I wasn't going to read about it. No cure, no point.

Twenty-three

Nana Lilith snuggled in beside me and Lolly on the couch, a print-out in her hands. I turned my head away, shutting my eyes. Nana was sneaky, though, and read it to me like I was a little kid again. It was nice. Relaxing and nice. Lolly liked being read to too.

According to the article my amygdala didn't like feeling threatened, so when it did it went nuts. 'Did you take that bit in, darling?' Nana asked.

'Yeah. No good trying to argue with your amygdala. It doesn't listen.' I gave a bit of a laugh. It sounded just like Mrs Nagel! She wasn't calm and rational either, and she totally didn't listen to reason.

There was more – all about finding a safe place. I stood up. 'Thanks, Nana. Okay to take Lolly for a walk?'

I had to escape. Obviously that so-called expert hadn't had to live in a place where nothing was safe. But Dr James Moran was okay. I almost felt safe in his office.

Lolly and I walked around the neighbourhood. People stop and chat when you go walking with a dog. It was nice, even when they mocked my Kiwi accent.

When I got back, Grandy and Nana Lilith gave me searching looks – it felt like they were scanning my brain to see what my amygdala was up to. I didn't mind; well, not too much. I figured they were entitled to be a bit on the hyper-alert side. Ha! Another quake term to throw around.

I curled up again on the sofa next to Lolly. 'That shrink – he looks like he's escaped from the bush, but he's okay. I don't even mind going back for another session.'

Which was just as well because Nana Lilith had twisted his arm to book me a few more appointments.

He was pretty keen on the safe place thing too. Yeah, I should have worked that out. He'd told me to read all about it, after all.

It turned out that Lolly was my safe place. I just had to keep the image in my head of her being a warm weight against my back in the night, of how she liked to cuddle up to me on the sofa and how she went berserk with glee if I said *walk*.

Dr James Moran gave me two *good girls* and told me to practise going back to those happy, safe feelings until they were good and solid in my head. 'Whenever there's a trigger, like another quake or hearing a train or a plane, get your mind to take you to Lolly and the feelings around her. And don't beat yourself up if you're not always a hundred per cent successful. You'll get better with practice.'

He made me practise deep breathing too. Breathe in, hold for three seconds, breathe out slowly. He reckoned that would haul my amygdala back by its toenails whenever it decided to take off into the stratosphere.

I knew I'd get plenty of chances to practise when I went back to Christchurch – the aftershocks were still frequent and some of them were severe. Joanne moaned about them every time she messaged me. I passed the news on to Katie and Shona, but one of Katie's answers surprised me. *Nelson's cool. Fab beaches. But I'd rather be in Christchurch. My city is changing and I'm not there to see what's happening.*

They wanted to know how I was doing. *I'm getting counselling!! Seems to be helping.*

I got the surprise of my life – Matt messaged. *Sent u awesome book.*

Me: *You've read an actual book???*

Matt: *Yep. X2*

Me: *It's about rugby, right?*

Matt: *Yes and no. Read it.*

It arrived three days later. I held the parcel for a few seconds before I even attempted opening it. I so didn't want to read a rugby book. Nana handed me a pair of scissors. A note written in Matt's scrawl fell out. *JK best winger ever. Read it.*

What? The book was *All Blacks Don't Cry*, by John Kirwan.

I gaped at it and just shook my head. Matt had to have lost a marble or two. Grandy picked it up. 'I've been wanting to read this. Great bloke, JK. He's done a good thing in talking about depression.'

The light went on in my head, along with a big fat question: was Matt finding life not so sweet too?

I read the book. Then I read it again.

Me: *Thanx.*

Matt: *When you back? Da gang going to gap-fill where my house used to be.*

Me: *Dunno. When you starting?*

Matt: *Waiting for u. That bossy little Imelda. And leo henry millie jess etc etc*

Me: (typing with grin on face) *Soon. Be back soon.*

We looked after Lolly for a week and a bit. When her ma and pa got home she was all over them. I felt betrayed and abandoned until she ran to sit beside me where I was curled up in a chair. There wasn't really room for me and a Doberman, but she made it work by taking over the whole of my lap.

'Come back and visit anytime,' they said, but I knew we wouldn't. The Sunshine Coast was quite a way from Lolly's house.

I stayed with my grandparents in their eighth-floor apartment for another week. I got lots of practise at amygdala hijack control every time I got in the lift or a truck went past when we were in town. Mostly it worked.

My friends asked what I was up to. *Shopping? Swimming? Theme parks?*

Nah. Am facing down the demons, doing deep breathing and pretending I've got a Doberman.

Joanne and Freya wrote news about school and messages flew around about gap-filling where Matt's house used to be. Henry wanted a swimming pool. Leo wanted a basketball hoop. Imelda wanted a family of gnomes. Millie: *Yes to gnomes. Maybe to hoop. Ha ha to pool. Matt wants orange flowers. Says they'll keep his mother away. Go figure!!*

There were things to look forward to. It was time to go back.

Author's note

I was born in Inglewood, Taranaki, but my mother was born in Christchurch and grew up there. I attended Christchurch Teachers' College in 1968 and there were earthquakes during that year. The worst one was the magnitude 7.1 Īnangahua quake that struck on the opposite side of the island, the West Coast, just before five-thirty in the morning. It woke me and my flatmates and I remember it was frightening. I just froze and hoped the house would stop shaking. We never felt entirely safe with the brick chimney that rose up through the middle of our flat after that. But Christchurch was fortunate as there was very little damage, unlike in the communities on the West Coast where the quake was centred.

On 4 September 2010 a devastating earthquake hit Christchurch at 4:35 a.m. I live in Wellington and I'd woken just after that time and turned on the radio. I found it hard to take in what I was hearing. A magnitude 7.1 quake had hit Christchurch? *Christchurch?* Wellington was the city with the shaky reputation. I listened in growing horror as people rang in with questions. *Was it okay to light candles? No, because there could be leaking gas.* The callers told awful stories of going outside to check on neighbours – but falling waist deep into a hole filled with liquefaction.

Because the quake had hit during the night when

people were at home in bed, nobody was directly killed, even though the damage was severe and would take months or years to repair. The entire country was relieved that people were safe and we did what we could to help. We learnt new words too – liquefaction was the top of the list. 'Munted' became the word of the moment to describe the broken city.

Repairs were well underway when the next big quake hit the region at 12.51p.m. on the afternoon of 22 February 2011. Although this quake wasn't as powerful as the September one, it caused more damage because it was shallower, just 5 kilometres below the surface whereas the September quake was at a depth of 11 kilometres. The ground acceleration (shaking) in February was more severe. This time, people were killed. It was a terrible time for Christchurch and the entire country.

I was in Christchurch later that year to do some school visits. Nothing was familiar. The Christchurch Cathedral was no longer a landmark. A local friend drove me around and needed to use a GPS because all the street names had fallen down, plus so many roads were closed because they were damaged or being repaired that it was easy to lose our way. She showed me the white chair memorial – 185 chairs all painted white to commemorate the 185 lives lost.

We saw the temporary new cathedral, dubbed the 'Cardboard Cathedral' because 98 heavy-duty cardboard tubes were used in its construction. We got out of the car to walk up to the cordoned-off 'Red Zone' and look through the wire barricade at the remains of the original cathedral. My friend stood there, tears falling. This was her city, her ruined city. She said she was looking at its devastated heart.

I gave a writing workshop to Avonside Girls' High School (AGHS) students during that visit. My mother had been a student – and head girl – at Avonside Girls' High School so I wanted the fictional character of Lyla to also go to that school. The students were still site-sharing with Burnside High School on the other side of the city from their own damaged school and because it was winter, the girls didn't get home until after dark. My abiding memory of all the students I met was their determination to keep going. The teachers were so concerned for their students, so focused on keeping things as normal as possible, even though many of the teachers, like their students, were living in homes that let in the rain and cold. Many homes had been completely destroyed and some people were having to make multiple moves as emergency and temporary housing became available.

There was so much disruption, so much destruction. One morning we drove past rows of suburban shops with their top-floor front walls missing so that all the world could see inside. In the afternoon when we drove back, there was only empty land. The whole site had been cleared.

Six years on, Christchurch is still in recovery. People are still trying to sort out insurance claims and are still trying to get their damaged houses properly repaired.

The cathedral is still sad and broken, roads are still being mended. But the city is full of street art – huge paintings on walls. Greenery and flowers pop up in empty spaces. There's a feeling of hope and there's energy in the air.

Timeline

2010 4 September 04:35 NZST (New Zealand Standard Time) A magnitude 7.1 earthquake strikes New Zealand's South Island. The epicentre is 37 km west of Christchurch near Darfield. Central Canterbury, especially Christchurch, incurs structural damage but there are no fatalities. More than 351 aftershocks are recorded.

In the days that follow, Sam Johnson starts a Facebook event called the 'Student Base for Earthquake Clean Up' to remove liquefaction from Christchurch. The Reserve Bank's initial estimate of recovery and rebuild costs is NZ$5 billion.

2011 22 February At 12:51 NZST a magnitude 6.3 aftershock lasting approximately 10 seconds strikes the Canterbury region. The epicentre is 2 km west of Lyttelton, just 10 km south-east of the Christchurch Central Business District (CBD). The shallow quake creates unprecedented ground shaking and is felt as far north as Tauranga and at Invercargill in the south.

Within minutes of the quake about 300 million tonnes of ice falls from the Tasman Glacier, located 200 km from the epicentre.

The National Crisis Management Centre is immediately activated to manage public response to the earthquake. The Mayor of Christchurch City declares a level 3 state of emergency. Hundreds of people are trapped in building rubble as hundreds more attempt to flee the devastation. Christchurch Hospital's emergency department treats 231 patients within the first hour post-earthquake.

A 'Red Zone' is quickly established in Christchurch CBD. Many buildings are cordoned off and widespread liquefaction begins to crack roads, swallow vehicles and rupture water and sewer pipes.

The Canterbury Television Building (CTV) collapses and catches fire. The Pyne Gould Corporation Building (PGC) housing 200 workers also falls. The spire and upper tower section of the Christchurch Cathedral collapse.

At 13:04 NZST a magnitude 5.8 aftershock hits Christchurch, followed by another aftershock measuring 5.9 at 14:50 NZST.

Emergency shelters are set up in Hagley Park. Power and water supply is cut off to 80% of the city. The eastern suburbs and Avon River environs are the hardest hit, with Lyttelton and New Brighton deemed unliveable. Christchurch Airport is closed to all but emergency flights.

Sam Johnson and over 2500 volunteers join with the University of Canterbury Students' Association to create the University of Canterbury Student Volunteer Army.

23 February Prime Minister John Key declares a national state of emergency as fatalities reach around 75. More than 1000 New Zealand Defence Force personnel lead the largest-ever rescue and recovery operation on home soil. Urban Search and Rescue and Disaster Victim Identification teams arrive from Australia, Japan, Singapore, the United Kingdom and the United States. The last survivor is pulled from the rubble.

The Student Volunteer Army joins thousands of people in the removal of over 200 000 tonnes of liquefaction silt.

A temporary mortuary is set up at Burnham Military Camp.

25 February Death toll reaches 115 with 228 people missing and many thousands injured.

Recovery operations continue with a focus on the CTV building and the Christchurch Cathedral site. Nine aftershocks measuring between 3.1 and 3.8 are recorded.

Christchurch Airport reopens as hundreds of Cantabrians leave the city.

Power is restored to 75% of the city but water and sewerage systems remain compromised.

March The official earthquake toll is 185 with 115 people perishing in the CTV building, 18 in the PGC building, 36 in the central city, 12 in the suburbs and 4 associated deaths. 81 international students and staff from King's Education died in the CTV building. More than 6000 people, including 220 major trauma cases, have been treated at Christchurch Hospital since the quake.

Prime Minister John Key announces that an estimated 100 000 houses have liquefaction damage and 10 000 are to be demolished. 163 primary and secondary schools remain closed including Avonside Girls' High School. 4879 Christchurch students enrol in other schools across New Zealand.

18 March Tens of thousands of people, including the Duke of Cambridge, attend the National Christchurch Memorial

Service at Hagley Park, where the names of the 185 victims are read out.

13 June A magnitude 6.3 earthquake, part of a prolonged aftershock sequence, occurs inland south-east of Christchurch. It affects about 400 000 people, with 46 people injured and widespread gas leaks and soil liquefaction. More than 100 additional buildings are now beyond repair. Christchurch Cathedral suffers further damage as the rose window in the west wall collapses. Experts believe this aftershock will increase construction costs by approximately NZ$6 billion. The Christchurch population year-to-date has fallen by 2.4% as 10 000 people relocate.

2012 Many schools reopen and Avonside Girls' High School students return to the school's original site.

397 025 tonnes of silt has now been cleared from Christchurch City. More than 90% of properties in Greater Christchurch suffer some earthquake damage. The Reserve Bank's revised repair and rebuilding estimate is NZ$20 billion. Canterbury Earthquake Recovery Authority suggests the rebuild plus improvements may well cost NZ$30 billion.

2013 The government purchases the CTV and PGC sites and makes a commitment to consult with the bereaved families over development plans. Cordons are finally lifted from the entire city.

2014 24 July Construction begins on a transitional cathedral in Christchurch.

15 August A dedication service for the transitional 'Cardboard Cathedral' designed by Japanese architect Shigeru Ban is held in Christchurch.

2015 February 1240 buildings in the four avenues of the Christchurch CBD have been demolished since the September 2010 earthquakes.

2015 November Ground-breaking (sod turning) ceremony announces the commencement of construction work on the Canterbury Earthquake National Memorial.

2017 21 February The Canterbury Earthquake National Memorial is unveiled to the bereaved families with a ceremony led by Ngāi Tahu representatives.

22 February Thousands of people attend the public opening of the Canterbury Earthquake National Memorial on the sixth anniversary of New Zealand's worst natural disaster since 1931.

Glossary

chuff bottom; behind; butt
dairy small neighbourhood corner shop
fanzone an area away from a sport venue (stadium) where people who don't have tickets to a game can be part of a crowd watching the game on huge screens
kapa haka the name for Māori performing arts, meaning to form a row (kapa) and dance (haka). Kapa haka is an emotional and powerful combination of singing, dancing, expression and movement
kia kaha be strong
korowai a Māori cloak made from traditional materials such as flax and feathers; a symbol of honour
liquefaction occurs when shaking from an earthquake causes loose soils to lose strength and act as a liquid
marae open area in front of a wharenui; the word 'marae' also has the meaning of generosity and sharing
munted broken; wrecked; busted
Rūaumoko god of earthquakes in Māori mythology
scarper run away

sprog baby or young child
te waiora the healing waters
tihei mauri ora let there be life
verge grassy strip on side of road; nature strip
wharenui meeting house

Find out more about ...

Christchurch earthquakes of 2010–11

https://www.britannica.com
Search for 'Christchurch earthquakes of 2010–2011 (New Zealand)'

22 February earthquake

https://www.youtube.com
Search for 'Christchurch Earthquake 2011'
Search for 'Christchurch Earthquake before and after'
Search for 'Liquefaction and Road Damage'

https://www.christchurchdailyphoto.com
Select 'February 2011' under 'Archives'

http://www.showusyourlongdrop.co.nz

Urban Search and Rescue Teams

https://earthquake-report.com
Search for 'rescue efforts continue to save lives'

Sessions, Laura. *Quake Dogs*, Random House, New Zealand, 2013

Student Volunteer Army

www.sva.org.nz

Cardboard Cathedral

https://www.theurbandeveloper.com
Search for 'Cardboard Cathedral'

National Dedication & Civic Commemoration Service 2017

https://www.youtube.com
Search for 'Families attend Chch earthquake memorial unveiling'

McKeever, Carol. *The Butterfly and the Earthquake*, First Edition Ltd., Wellington, New Zealand, 2011

Acknowledgements

So many people generously gave their time to tell me their experiences. I'm particularly grateful to staff and students of Avonside Girls' High School: principal Sue Hume, librarian Kaylene Moore, English Department staff, and ex-students Jessamie Davidson and Aleisha Cotterill (who were both in their first year at AGHS in 2011). My heartfelt thanks to Linley Earnshaw, librarian at Christchurch Girls' High School for her stories and for checking the finished manuscript to ensure that it truly reflected people's experiences. I'm very grateful to Belynda Smith who generously shared her stories. Police officers took the time to give me a picture of what it was like in the aftermath of the quake. A member of the police communications staff was especially helpful as she was stationed in Christchurch for a week a few days after the February quake.